EMPTY PLACES

KATHY CANNON WIECHMAN

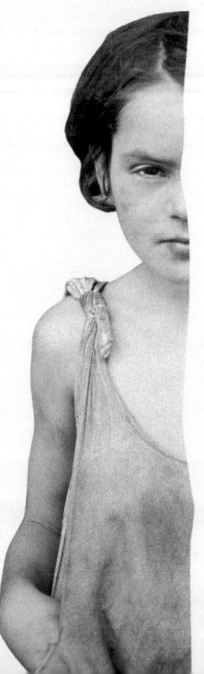

EMPTY
PLACES

CALKINS CREEK
AN IMPRINT OF HIGHLIGHTS
Honesdale, Pennsylvania

Calkins Creek
An Imprint of Highlights
815 Church Street
Honesdale, Pennsylvania 18431

Printed in the United States of America
ISBN: 978-1-62979-451-8
ISBN: 978-1-62979-560-7 (e-book)
Library of Congress Control Number: 2015953544

First edition
The text of this book is set in Janson.
Design by Barbara Grzeslo
Production by Sue Cole
10 9 8 7 6 5 4 3 2 1

Dedicated to the memory of
Helen Sargeant Wiechman and
Mary Wiechman Nies

CHAPTER 1

HARLAN COUNTY

If you'da rode into Harlan County, Kentucky, that June in a shiny new 1932 Packard, you'da seen hickories, oaks, and maples leafed out with the promise of shady places to rest and listen to birdsong.

If you'da got close enough to set in one of them shady spots, you'da heard the chug of engines pulling coal cars that squealed on aged tracks. You'da heard swear-words of miners and seen coal dust that clung to their faces, filled their pores, and caused their lungs to heave out deep, retching coughs.

But even if you'da been close as a tick on a dog, you wouldn'ta heard the secrets each body kept, secrets not even told in whispers—secrets about my mama.

Secrets and gossip spread through coal camps like Smoke Ridge the way a fever does, keeping folks talking. Until new gossip seeps into their lives. Old gossip, like stale bread, is all but forgotten when there's fresh bread to chew on.

When Hard Times hit Smoke Ridge, most folks talked about money and how they didn't have none. But some old gossip come back around again and again, floating to the surface like dead fish. And smelt near as bad.

Whispers about Daddy wasn't fresh. And they wasn't secret. Each body, hound dog, and woods critter knew about Daddy. The string of words following Ray Cutler's name was sure to include *no-account, God-forsaken*—and *drunk*. Folks said Daddy was so full of liquor most times, he ought'a have a cork in his mouth.

I'd heard *those* whispers since I was no bigger'n spring corn. I'da had to be deaf as a stump not to have heard them. Onliest reason they was said in whispers was to make sure us Cutlers knew we wasn't fit to be spoke of out loud.

Ever'body knew liquor and spirits of any kind was unlawful, but it weren't Daddy breaking the law that got folks bothered up. After all, lots of Smoke Ridge miners drank, but none of t'others seemed to git quite as mean and wrathful like Daddy got when he drank. So folks talked. And looked down on us.

Secrets about Mama was different. I didn't rightly know there was any secrets until that June I turned thirteen. By then, I scarce remembered I'd ever had a mama. I was six when she left.

That June, I was in the company Dry Goods store, hoping to find marked-down fabric. My older sister Raynelle wanted to make a dress for Blissie, the youngest Cutler, who was growing faster'n a summer weed. I looked through stacks of dress goods, my hand in my pocket, clasping the steel coin Raynelle had give me. My fingers stroked its raised writing and the tip of my fingernail poked into the squiggle that was stamped clean through the middle of it. The squiggle was the letter *S*. *S* for Smoke Ridge. Not United States real American money—this was company scrip. The only kind of money we ever saw in Smoke Ridge.

A piece of pink-flowered cotton peeked from under several bolts of shirting, a color that would match the bloom in Blissie's cheeks. I scooched down between the shelves to pry it from the bottom of the stack.

From my frog-like position, I heard the tinkle of the bell over the door, and Miz Myrtle Henry's voice threw out a "Hey there" to Miz Sparks, who worked the store's counter for the coal company. I stayed where I was, out of eye-shot of Miz Henry, but I heard ever' word as she sized up and cut down ever'body in Smoke Ridge.

It didn't take long for her to git around to Daddy—and to us. "Crying shame Ray Cutler ain't suitable husband stock. Those Cutler young'uns ought'a have a woman around to look after 'em and keep 'em clean."

I looked down at the gravy stain on my faded dress, but the stain was old and the dress fresh-washed. I had ironed it myself.

"Their mama would have a conniption if she seen 'em now," Miz Henry went on.

"That no-account father of theirs don't care a spit about 'em," Miz Sparks said back. "Likely one day they'll foller the same road Ada did."

Ada. A name so like my own. But I hadn't heard Mama's name spoke out loud in such a long time, it startled my ears.

None of us Cutler young'uns knew exactly which road Mama took when she left. All's we knew was what Daddy said back when Blissie was jist two. "Your mama done run off. Don't rightly know if she'll be comin' back."

And she never had.

9

CHAPTER 2

MYRTLE HENRY

Hearing Miz Sparks say Mama's name caused feelings to gurgle up inside me. I knew Raynelle was named for Daddy, and two years later, Pick was named *Pickens* for Mama's kin. But I got the honor of carrying Mama's name as part of mine. *Adabel.*

By the time Blissie come along, they must'a run out of folks to honor. Blissie is her own self. With her own name. And a sweetness that makes folks smile and forgit she's a Cutler.

I held my breath, waiting to hear more words about Mama, but Miz Henry's gossip moved on to Mr. Putney's nephew, who was expected to come for a visit afore the end of the month.

But Mama'd been stirred up in my mind. Untalked-about for such a long time, she was no more'n an empty place in our lives.

I tried to recall her face, but there was no picture in my mind to summon. I knew Raynelle resembled her, with brown hair and brown eyes. And something inside me believed that Blissie's sweetness come from her. It sure didn't come from Daddy.

My brother Pick and me was cursed with Daddy's red hair, which folks said carried a bad temper. Daddy had that temper for sure. But I worked hard to keep holt of mine.

There had to be more in my memory of Mama than glimpses of my sisters, but I couldn't find one speck of it. No matter how hard I tried.

My legs was tired of crouching, and I shifted my weight a speck jist as Miz Sparks whispered something to Miz Henry. The only word I could make out was *Grayson*, but Miz Henry's reaction to the name was clear as daylight.

"That varmint!" she said. "S'posed to be selling insurance, but spends most of his time poking his nose into what don't concern him."

"Don't fret," Miz Sparks said. "He don't never stay long in Smoke Ridge. He lives up in Letcher County someplace, and always seems to have real money to spend. Not jist Smoke Ridge scrip."

Miz Henry clicked her tongue and changed the subject.

My feet plumb went to sleep and sent prickly feelings up my legs by the time Miz Henry chose a bolt of blue linen for Miz Sparks to measure out. I could'a chose it for her the minute she walked in. Blue linen always creased across Myrtle Henry's lap whenever she stood up to throw out an *Amen* to Pastor Justice's sermons. I cain't remember her in any other Sunday color, setting in a front pew with a look on her face that told ever'body she was better than they was.

I waited for her to leave the store, but she stood jawing with Miz Sparks until I knew I had to pry out that bolt of pink fabric and suck down my pride. I tugged and tugged, wiggling it back and forth, edging it out from under the bolts of shirting an inch at a time.

The cloth came free as I pulled so hard I landed on my backside and fell against another shelf. The shelf wobbled and dislodged a box of thimbles that overturned. They plinked to the floor around me like bells in search of a melody.

I scrambled to my feet, knowing full well Miz Sparks would have a tongue-lashing for me. And Miz Henry would have more new Cutler gossip to spread around Smoke Ridge.

Without a glance in their direction, I tore out of that store like a muddy hound chased with a broom. Raynelle was goin' be horn-mad when I got home without fabric, but I couldn't face those old biddies. Not and hold back my redheaded temper.

CHAPTER 3

JANE LOUISE

I fled into the hard-packed dirt street and zipped past Jane Louise Heckathorn, who was fixing to head into the store. Jane Louise was closest to a friend I had, but I didn't stop.

"Adabel, wait!" she called.

"Not now," I said betwixt my teeth.

But Jane Louise follered me, though she dropped further and further behind. She wasn't the kind to hurry, believing a girl's forehead should never be dotted with sweat. I never give thought to such things and didn't slow down, even when I seen my brother Pick walking towards me.

I sidestepped to skirt around him, but that ran me headlong into the chest of Norris Shortwell.

"Nice running into you, Adabel," he said, and wrapped his arms around me, pinning my arms at my sides.

I tried to squirm free of his grip, but he didn't let go.

"Don't set her free until she burns off some of whatever got her het up," Pick warned him.

I stewed for a minute and caught my breath afore I stomped down hard on Norris's foot. His grip loosed a mite, but he hung on, and I felt his breathing aside my ear.

13

"For such a skinny critter, your sister's meaner'n a dang pant'er," he told Pick with a laugh. I kicked his shin, and afore he had time to recover, I lit out, heading for the stand of pines surrounding Mr. Webster's outhouse.

I stopped in the shade and shadows, where the scent of pine was stronger than the backhouse smell, and watched as Jane Louise reached the boys. I knew she was fixing to change right in front of me, like a tadpole turning into a frog.

Jane Louise always changed when boys was around. Her voice got whispery, her eyes got fluttery, and her lips formed a pout that turned boys into confounded lugheads. From where I stood, I couldn't hear what she said to 'em, but I watched a performance I had witnessed all too often.

And I wasn't the only one who seen it. Jist outside Mr. Webster's Grocery, him and Mr. Grayson, the insurance peddler Miz Sparks had spoke of, stopped whatever they was talking about to watch Jane Louise and the boys.

Norris seemed to git three inches taller with Jane Louise in front of him. His lips flapped like a loose boot sole. But like as not, he didn't say shucks worth hearing.

Most folks called Norris by the nickname of Shovel, and not on account'a he could shovel verbal manure better than most—which he could. But on account'a him and my brother being friends since they was babies. Always together, Pick and Shovel.

Even that brother of mine that Teacher Bromley said was smart enough to be *somebody* someday, become a half-wit in the presence of Jane Louise's charms.

Me and Jane Louise got along jist fine, but the way she behaved with boys confounded me. She claimed to keep company with Corky Danfield, whose daddy was a boss at the Smoke Ridge Mine, but she still shamelessly teased and flirted with ever' boy in Harlan County.

I couldn't watch another minute of it. I headed home, without fabric for Blissie's dress or one shred of dignity.

My mind went back to those harpies at the Dry Goods. Did they know what made Mama leave Harlan County all them years ago? And did they know where she went?

CHAPTER 4

THE OLD HOUSE

The biddies at the store had my mind churning about Mama, who I hadn't thunk of in quite a spell. She was never spoke of at home on account'a Daddy. We never knew what might rile him, and we tried right hard not to find out.

On the path towards home, the word *Why?* sounded in my head with ever' step. Why did she leave? Why couldn't I remember?

I stopped quick-like. I had passed the old fork that my feet used to know so well. Scurrying back, I took that old path and come over a rise to a house I thunk about sometimes, though I tried not to.

You might think Mama left on account'a she got tired of living the poor life like we done. But back when Mama left, we lived in this good-sized house on a patch of land with vegetable gardens enough to feed us hearty ever' day of the year. We even had a mess of chickens and a pig. Back afore the Hard Times.

Raynelle could recollect when Granny and Granddaddy Cutler owned this house. Mama, Daddy, Pick, and her lived here with 'em. She said she was four years old when Granddaddy sold the house to Daddy, his only son. How on earth Raynelle could remember what happened when she was four bewildered me. I couldn't even remember Mama.

16

I looked around at trees and brush. Last year's dead leaves moldered amidst what was once a vegetable garden. Surely Mama had tended that garden, pulling weeds and planting new life into its soil.

I counted on my fingers the seven years Mama'd been gone. We'd still lived in this house for dang near six of them years, so of course I remembered the house. But Mama was an empty place in my mind.

I blew out my breath and meandered over to the garden shed. It no longer had a door. Sunlight shone through a hole in its roof onto its dirt floor, where weeds had taken root. Weeds was all that flourished in Harlan County anymore.

I walked right up to the house, scraped dirt off a windowpane, and peeked in. Other than a broken bedstead in the corner, the room was empty. A room me and my sisters had shared. Recollections of jokes and laughter with Raynelle in that room flitted through my mind, us talking about silly things and jabbering on and on about ever'thing. And nothing. Back on those rare days when she felt like my sister.

But it wasn't our house no more, and it seemed we didn't hardly laugh at all now. And Raynelle was more like a mama than a sister. But she wasn't Mama. Mama was gone. Gone from Smoke Ridge. Gone from my memory.

I moved to the front porch, where a dusty *For Sale or Rent* sign leaned against the siding. I recalled a rocking chair that used to set here. Surely Mama had rocked in that chair, maybe with Blissie in her arms, but I couldn't remember none of it. What was wrong with me?

I plunked down on the top step. Years of weather had grayed the steps considerable, and the house's white paint had peeled like birch bark. But being there brought back a sense of the way things was afore Hard Times wore us down like the dirt road into Smoke Ridge.

Daddy always said that ever'body in Harlan County lived a "hand-to-mouth life." But in the past year or so, our hands become emptier and the distance to our mouths seemed longer.

I truly hated being poor. It didn't make sense that we lived crammed in a tiny box of a shanty when nobody lived in this big house. I jumped up and give the *For Sale or Rent* sign a sturdy kick, and heard the tinkle of broken glass. Behind the sign, I found three empty Mason jars with lids, one of them now busted into five large pieces.

I picked up a busted piece with the lid still attached, avoiding a jagged shard of glass sticking out like a giant's tooth. Not one speck of dust or dirt tainted that glass.

I took a sniff and the reason flew right up my nose and into my head. I couldn't have lived with Daddy all these years and not known that smell. *Moonshine!*

Seemed like our old house had become a drop place for a moonshiner and his customer. And moonshiners could be nasty-tempered folks.

The wind picked up, causing a dogwood's leaves to shudder. A rustling sound come from the hemlock grove beyond the vegetable garden. A moonshiner? With a shotgun? A chill shivered down the back of my dress. I dropped the busted jar and scampered back to the fork and took the trail towards home, thoughts of Mama scared clean out'a my head.

CHAPTER 5

THE
SHANTY

"Stop being a scaredy-cat," I said to myself once I was a safe distance from the old house. Like as not, the sound in the hemlock grove had been the wind. I took a deep breath and headed home, crossing the board that spanned the creek and follering the trail up the hill through the woods.

Coming from the trees behind our shanty, I stopped and stared. After the old house, the shanty seemed smaller than ever. Its three rooms was more like one room and two half-rooms. And it weren't truly ours. It belonged to the Smoke Ridge Mine Company, which was owned by Mr. Clarence Putney, who took the rent out of Daddy's pay.

Lonesome dozed on the back porch, but he opened one eye to let me know he was doing his job. We only had a couple chickens and a small garden patch, but we needed ever' egg, potato, green bean, cabbage, tomato, and ear of corn that grew there. That dog made sure no greedy hand swiped nothing when we wasn't looking.

Last year, after the A&P in Evarts was broke into twice and its shelves picked clean, Daddy brung home the mutt puppy.

I patted Lonesome's head as I walked past and stepped into the house, where the smell of bean soup filled the space that served as kitchen, eating room, sitting room, and even Pick's bedroom. Daddy was at work in the mine that afternoon, and Raynelle stirred soup at the stove. I noticed the way her hand held the wood spoon, easing it through the soup. Surely I'd watched Mama cook when I was a young'un, but when I tried to recall it, all's I saw was Raynelle.

"Did you find dress goods?" she asked over her shoulder.

I shook my head and lied. "Pickings was poor for what you give me to spend." I plinked the steel coin on the table.

The scrip Mr. Putney paid Daddy with, after he took out the rent, was good only at the company stores. All two of 'em. And at the cookhouse, where miners who didn't have someone at home to cook for 'em could grab a meal.

"It's all we kin afford," Raynelle said, "at least until work picks up."

Mine shifts was cut to two days a week the last year or so. Banner Fork Mine near Wallins Creek, a mine owned by Mr. Henry Ford, closed down completely last fall. If Mr. Ford couldn't keep a mine running, what chance did Mr. Putney have? I reckoned we was lucky Smoke Ridge Mine was still open and Daddy had a job.

When the Citizens National Bank down in Harlan closed in January, I didn't understand what that had to do with *us*. We didn't have no money in the bank anyhow. Pick said one body's Hard Times becomes ever'body's Hard Times after a spell.

"The dress Blissie wore to church last week used to be yours," Raynelle told me, "and mine afore that. It's threadbare and too tight. There's old ones of yours still packed away, but ever' one has some kind of stain or t'other." She turned from the stove to scold me with her eyes. "You never was a neat child."

"I ain't a child no more."

"But you still ain't neat. Blissie's goin' need a proper dress afore school starts in September, and without a sewing machine, it'll likely take me the rest of the summer to make it."

Blissie was the only Cutler young'un who still went to school. The rest of us had to do our share of work at home. Daddy never seemed to be around often enough to tend to the garden or house like other daddies did. And when he was home, he was seldom sober enough to walk straight, much less hoe a garden or patch a shed.

Me, I never truly missed school, but Pick seemed to crave it like Daddy craved drink. He still stopped by the schoolhouse to visit with Teacher Bromley. He swore he was goin' fill his head with learning and not work in the mines like Daddy.

Pick would be sixteen next year, old enough to git a job. But the Hard Times had dried up all kinds of work. He'd be lucky not to be one of them pencil-sellers on a Wallins street corner.

"Take a look in that trunk yonder," Raynelle said. "Maybe I kin make over one of Mama's old dresses for Blissie."

Mama's dresses? That was the second time in one day I'd heard Mama spoke of. Why hadn't I known she left dresses behind? Why couldn't I remember her?

CHAPTER 6

BREAD WITH BEAN SOUP

It wasn't a big trunk, and it'd set under the back window for as long as we'd lived here. I'd tried to open it once, but it was locked, so I never give it much thought except when Raynelle made me dust it ever' Saturday.

I recollected Blissie setting on it once in the old house, on account of Pastor Justice come to dinner and we didn't have enough chairs.

And I recalled a stray cat Blissie drug home last winter that liked to sprawl atop that trunk in the afternoon sunlight. Leastways, for the few days Kitty stayed with us. One night, stupefied by drink, Daddy tripped over Kitty in the dark. Between the cat's screeches and yowls and Daddy's swear-words, the entire house was awake to see Daddy fling the critter out the door. Blissie looked for "poor Kitty" for near a week, but none of us ever seen it again.

You might'a thunk Blissie would'a been crossways with Daddy over that, but not Blissie. She reported to Daddy on her fruitless searches and comforted him as though he missed Kitty as much as she done.

Today, I pulled the trunk out from the wall a mite to open it. Its hinges squeaked as I raised the lid. "I don't recollect this trunk ever being unlocked afore," I said.

Raynelle blushed. "Daddy caught me playing in Mama's dresses once when we was in the old house. He took to locking it after that. Said if'n Mama come home, she wouldn't want to find her dresses mussed and dirty."

"Daddy thunk Mama might come home?"

"I was jist a young'un then," Raynelle said. "We all know better now, don't we?"

Inside the trunk, a few folded dresses set right on top. I lifted out a brown one with a lace collar, its long old-fashioned skirt draping clean to the floor. I gently run my fingers along the yellowed lace, and in the corner of my mind I seen Mama, wearing that dress and calling my name.

But in an instant she was gone, and it was Raynelle's voice that asked, "What do ya think, Adabel? Kin I cut down an old dress of Mama's to fit Blissie?"

I tried to recall that picture of Mama, but it had vanished like fog in summer sun. "No, don't," I told Raynelle as I closed the trunk lid. "Ya might kin use the buttons, but them dresses is more out'a date than Mr. Webster's flowered suspenders."

Raynelle giggled. "Don't speak ill of the man who might be my father-in-law one day."

"Eww! Ya wouldn't really marry Luddy Webster, would ya?" I hoped she wouldn't marry nobody anytime soon. How would we ever git by without Raynelle?

"Why not? His daddy runs the Grocery. I could eat myself full three times a day and have food left over."

"What about when the Hard Times end? We'll eat good anyhow. And there you'll be, stuck married to Lughead Luddy. Prob'ly with a passel of plain-faced babies that look jist like their daddy."

"Lud ain't so plain. And a grocer's wife has a heap better life than a miner's wife. Lud treats me like a lady, which is more'n I can say for most boys in Smoke Ridge."

I didn't much care what boys thought, but I seen the way folks treated us. "They think we're poor as dirt and common as pig tracks," I said.

"The whole country's poor as dirt right now. And pigs ain't as common as they used to be. Look in that sack yonder afore you bad-mouth Lud."

The wax-paper sack held a loaf of store bread, the white-flour kind we hadn't been able to afford since the old house.

"It's moldy," I said.

"Jist on one end. I kin cut that off. It'll be good to have something filling with the bean soup tonight. I swear I'm sick to death of pinto beans, but what else kin a body feed a family on for three cents a pound?"

Raynelle's hair was coming loose from its pins and hung around the edges of her face like a fur scarf. The role of mother had been thrust on her when Mama left, and even at ten, she wore it like a seamstress-made dress. Seventeen now, she kept our little home tidy and watched our meager scrip.

I screwed up my courage to tell her about the pink-flowered fabric, but fell miles short of a full confession. "There *was* a pretty piece of marked-down cloth at the store. Might be if we wait a day or two, Miz Sparks'll mark it down a bit more."

But dress goods wasn't what I truly wanted to talk about. "Myrtle Henry was in the store, and her and Miz Sparks was chewing Daddy over."

"Some folks got nothing better to do." Raynelle tasted the soup, added a pinch of salt, and stirred.

I waited until I was sure she was listening. "Miz Sparks said maybe we'd leave someday like Mama done."

"And go where? To do what?" She tasted the soup again.

"I don't know." I watched her face close as I asked, "Where do you think Mama went? And to do what?"

"I pondered on that a thousand times in the past seven years. Wherever she went, she didn't take much with her."

"Do ya think she meant to come back? Or did she truly plan to leave forever?" A new thought hit me. "What if she come back and looked for us at the old house?"

"If she didn't come back in six years, it ain't likely she'd come back in the seventh. Now stop pestering with questions I cain't answer, and set the table for supper. Daddy'll come home tired and hungry."

Pick come through the door in time to hear them last words. "That beats the hound out'a him coming home drunk and mean," he said.

I thunk about the old house again. Daddy'd been drunk and mean plenty of times when we lived there, but I seemed to recall a time afore that. A time when Daddy seemed upstanding enough to invite Pastor Justice to dinner. A time when Daddy bounced Blissie on his knee and tickled her face with his beard. A time when a loving Daddy cared about his young'uns.

I couldn't recollect the order of things. Was it Daddy's drunken ways that drove Mama away? Or did Mama's leaving turn Daddy to drink?

CHAPTER 7

WEEDS, WATER, AND WARNING WORDS

Chores kept me busy ever' day. Lonesome watched me from the porch, as I pulled weeds from the vegetable patch. Over my shoulder, the corn was gitting tall, and I couldn't stop thinking about the taste of corn on the cob, cornbread, and corn pudd'n. It would be a likeable change from pinto beans. Maybe in a couple more weeks.

The same sun that would ripen the corn had hardened the ground. That hard ground made it seem like an underground critter pulled harder on his end of the weeds than I did on mine.

I fetched a bucket and stepped onto the porch to go inside for water. A porch plank creaked under my foot, and my mind thunk about Daddy, who was sleeping off last night's bender. The creek seemed a better idea. I trekked down the trail from the back of our house, hoping Daddy would be in a good mood when he woke up.

As I looked back up the hill, our shanty blended in with other weatherworn houses, cleaving to hillsides like fungus to a log. I could hear the *plunk, chunk!* sound of Pick splitting firewood beside the shanty. We didn't need a fire in the fireplace most summer nights, but sometimes Raynelle used it for cooking to save on coal.

As I neared the creek, I heard voices. And giggling.

I crept quiet along the trail, moving from tree to tree. Standing behind the sturdy trunk of a maple, I caught a glimpse of Raynelle's ever'day work dress. What was she doing down here by the creek?

She murmured quiet words, and I heard a male voice answer back. I peeked around the tree and tried to move closer. But my foot slid down the hill a mite, and nudged a stick that tapped a rock that sent a passel of other rocks to rolling into the creek with a splash.

"Adabel Cutler!" Raynelle hollered, and jumped to her feet. "Why in tarnation are you spying on me and Lud?"

I stepped out from behind my tree. After a few stammers, I said, "I jist come down to fetch water to loose up the garden." I held out the bucket as proof.

"Ain't you got water in your kitchen?" Lud asked, straightening his clothes and looking sheep-like.

I looked at Raynelle. "Daddy's asleep in there," I said.

Her eyes showed she understood, but Lud said, "If'n Ray Cutler is still sleeping off a snootful this time of day, the wrath of God won't wake him. Ya needn't be afeared of your own daddy."

"You're the one what ought'a be scared of him, Lud. 'Specially if he catches you down here kissing on my sister."

Raynelle blushed. "Adabel! Hush your mouth. Me and Lud was jist talking." But the blush that spread from her face to his told me different.

"No matter," I said. "If Daddy wakes up and finds you're off 'jist talking' with Lud, you best have good reasons for why."

She brushed off the back of her dress, looked a good-bye to Lud, and latched holt of my elbow. "Come on, Adabel. I'll go heat the soup for when Daddy wakes up."

I pulled away. "I still need to fetch water."

"Well, hurry on." She raised her chin and headed up the path like she was Queen of the Hills.

Lud watched her go. "See ya tomorrow?" he called after her.

She didn't turn around.

I planted my feet and looked Lud straight in the eye. "Ya best tread careful around my sister. If ya git into a tangle with Daddy, it might be the last tangle ya ever git in."

CHAPTER 8

PINK
FABRIC

Raynelle sent me to the Grocery for salt—and to see if the pink-flowered fabric at the Dry Goods had been marked down. It pained me a mite to lie to Raynelle and it pained me a heap to have to walk back into that store and face Miz Sparks.

Smoke Ridge wasn't a town, jist a coal camp. The Dry Goods set beside the Grocery, across from the cookhouse, Mr. Putney's office, and the blacksmith shop. At the far end stood the two-room school that doubled as a church one Sunday a month, when Pastor Justice drove over from Bell County to preach.

Beyond the school and down the road was the main entry to Smoke Ridge Mine. I couldn't see it from here, and Daddy didn't like us girls to go down there. But we could see the smudgy sky and hear loud blasts when miners used black powder to loose up the coal.

The mine itself went deep underground, reaching its tunnels into more rooms than any house atop the earth. Them rooms of coal set beneath places where folks walked ever' day. Ventilation shafts reached through hills, and fans sent dangerous gases out holes that dotted hillsides. We knew to keep clear of 'em.

Evenings, we heard whistles from trains that carried full cars of mined coal down to the coke ovens. Mornings, the trains rumbled back with empty cars, ready to be filled again.

Today, I readied myself to face Miz Sparks. I looked down to check my dress for spots and wrinkles. I wiped dust from my bare feet on a grassy place between the stores, even though I knew that two more steps would dirty 'em again. In a county full of coal miners, coal dust from their clothes dropped and settled on ever'thing.

When my feet was as clean as I could git 'em, I took a deep breath and stepped inside the store.

"Hey, Miz Sparks," I said, polite as you please. "I come to look at dress goods."

No one else was in the store, and I sauntered over to the pile of shirting where I seen the fabric two days ago. It wasn't there.

I scooched way down to git a better look under the shirting. A thimble on the floor peeked out from the edge of the shelf, reminding me of that clumsy girl I'd been when I'd knocked over the whole box of 'em. I swallowed back that reminder and glanced to the other side of the store. But them was all miners' things. Hats, boots, tools, lanterns, and flasks of carbide. Pink fabric would'a stood out like a woodpecker's red head.

I breathed deep and strolled myself up to the counter. "Miz Sparks, ma'am, I seen some pink cloth t'other day with flowers sprinkled on it. Ya still have it?"

She leaned behind the counter and hauled up the bolt I wanted. She held it with her thumb and one finger like it was a dirty diaper. "Is this the one ya mean?"

I sucked in an excited breath. "Yes, ma'am."

"It's less'n three yards and it's a mite soiled," she said, afore adding in a down-her-nose tone, "Seems some'un left it on the floor. Cain't imagine any decent person wanting soiled dress goods, but it's half off if you've a mind to buy it anyhow."

I give her a steel coin and pocketed smaller scrip coins she give me in change, happy for a bargain and hoping Raynelle could git out the dirt.

Miz Sparks handed me the fabric and waited for me to leave, but I couldn't. I'd been digging in my mind the past couple days like a miner putting in a hard day's work, trying to unearth memories of Mama. I had to keep digging.

"Miz Sparks." I aimed my question full-bore: "You remember my mama, don't ya?"

"'Course I do, Adabel. Your mama and me was good friends. A lovely woman, your mama."

Why did it pain me so that this sharp-tongued biddy had memories of my mama, when I couldn't find one scrap of her memory in my whole head?

"Ya heard from her recent?" I asked.

I had never mentioned Mama to Miz Sparks afore, and she forced the surprised look off her face afore she answered. "Why, no, I ain't."

"She don't never write to ya?"

"Your mama was never one much for writing."

"Do ya know where she is?"

"No, I certainly don't."

"Why do ya reckon that is, Miz Sparks, seeing's you was such good friends and all?"

She coughed and cleared her throat. "I . . . we . . . she . . .

You run along now, Adabel. I have work to do."

"Yes, ma'am. I reckon you need to sweep this floor afore more dress goods gits dirty." I snatched up the fabric and didn't light out, but walked out that door calm as you please with my nose jist a tad in the air.

The screen door hadn't banged shut yet when I near run into Mr. Grayson, the insurance peddler from Letcher County. As he passed me on his way into the store, his scornful look flattened my prideful feeling like a stomped-on blackberry.

CHAPTER 9

A GOOD
WOMAN

I walked into the Grocery as Myrtle Henry was paying Mr. Webster for a box of groceries.

"Ya want me to have my boy Lud tote this on up to your place, Myrtle?" Mr. Webster asked. "It's a mite heavy."

"No need to bother the boy," Miz Henry said. "I'll take half now and git the rest tomorrow."

I sucked in my breath and forced words out. "I kin tote it for ya, Miz Henry." Myrtle Henry had spoke about Mama those few days ago, and I reckoned she was another thread I could tug on.

But Myrtle's face got red and puckery. "I don't need *your* help." She near-about spat the words at me.

It might'a been the way she said the word *your*, like I was a thief who might steal her precious groceries. Or it might'a been the way Mr. Grayson's look had wilted me. But something dug into my skin and peppered my anger.

"Then carry your own dang groceries," I flung at her. "I was jist trying to be nice. But I don't reckon you'd know *nice* if it bit you on your big old nose."

She raised her chin and threw out a high-minded "Well!" afore she snatched up three cakes of yeast and a sack of sugar.

33

She stomped to the door and told Mr. Webster she'd be back tomorrow. Mr. Webster's screen door slammed with a *bang* and Myrtle Henry was gone.

Would I never learn to keep holt of my temper? That old hen was never goin' tell me anything about Mama now.

"Sorry," I mumbled to Mr. Webster, and looked down at my bare toes. "Daddy'll take a switch to my backside if'n he hears I was rude to Miz Henry."

"Don't trouble yourself none, Adabel." He winked at me. "It'll be our secret. Besides, she was rude first."

"I was fixing to ask her about my mama."

Mr. Webster looked around his store, but we was the onliest ones there. "What about your mama?" he said in a whisper.

"I jist want to know something about her."

"What kind of something?"

"Any kind of something. I scarce remember her."

"I kin tell you your mama was a good woman."

"Miz Sparks says so, but what was so good about her?"

"Ain't it enough to know she was good?"

I shook my head. "Would it be enough if'n it was *your* mama, and ya couldn't recall a lick about her?"

Mr. Webster rubbed his chin. "Your mama and my wife, Patsy, was friends. Surely ya recall that."

I didn't recollect Miz Webster neither, but I didn't say so.

Mr. Webster leaned forward on his counter and talked low. "Nigh on eight years ago, my wife, Patsy, heard about a man down near Wallins who lost his wife. Him and his daddy was both miners and both ailing. Patsy and Ada traipsed down there to cook a few meals for 'em. That's what kind of women they was.

And that's all ya really need to know. Kin I git something for ya?"

"Salt, please."

When I stepped from the store, I seen my brother Pick on the Dry Goods porch talking to Mr. Grayson. I wondered for a minute what them two was talking about, but I didn't tote the question home with me. I already carried a bolt of pink cloth, a package of salt, and a more important question: *Why would a woman kind enough to cook for sick miners pick up and leave her family?*

CHAPTER 10

BLISSIE
AND
LULA

Blissie's face beamed when she seen the pink-flowered fabric. "Kin ya git it clean, Raynelle? If ya cain't, put the dirty spots in back where I cain't see 'em, and I'll wear it anyhow."

"I think it'll wash. Don't you worry none. As long as I'm heating up a wash pot, ya ought'a let me toss in Lula."

Blissie hugged her filthy rag doll tight against her chest. "Lula ain't clothes for washing," she said. "She's a baby."

"Babies need baths," I said. "We kin give Lula a bath."

It was never easy to pry Lula away from Blissie. That doll was near as attached as her fingers and toes. Had been for as long as I could remember. Raynelle had replaced her stuffing and repaired her seams countless times.

I hadn't thought about it afore now, but if Blissie'd had that doll since she was a baby, the original seams and stitched-on mouth and eyes must have been Mama's handiwork. I suddenly had a new respect for that old doll. We'd have to be right careful with its bath.

Blissie rubbed Lula's cloth hand against her lip, the way she always done when she was troubled or thinking hard. I'd always found that habit disgusting on account'a the doll was so dirty, but now I wished I had something Mama made to hold close to my own face.

I dipped the doll gently into a pan of suds whilst Blissie watched anxiously. "Don't hurt her none, Adabel."

"Don't worry." The pan set on a small washstand. It wobbled a mite, but that could'a been on account'a uneven porch planks as much as a short washstand leg.

After Lula's light scrubbing, I emptied the wash pan and filled it with clean water. I dipped Lula into it, squeezing soap from her until she stopped squirting out suds.

I held her up for Blissie's inspection. "See," I said, "she come through jist fine."

Blissie's smile was restored, and she traipsed behind me toting two clothespins as I carried her doll to the clothesline that zigzagged back and forth betwixt our shanty and the one next door.

I didn't realize Daddy was leaning up against the house until too late. A Mason jar tipped to his lips was near empty, and his eyes showed he was already slop-faced.

"What mischief you girls up to now?" Daddy's words come out slurred and angry.

"No mischief, Daddy," Blissie said. "Me and Adabel just give Lula a bath."

"Ya's playing dolls when there's work to be done?" The roared question made Blissie jump. She grabbed Lula from me and run around the corner of the house.

Daddy follered in a hurried stagger. "Ya's too old to be playing with dolls anyhow."

Me and Raynelle often said the same thing to one another, but neither of us could bear to part Blissie from her beloved Lula.

I come around the corner jist in time to see tears in Blissie's eyes as she disappeared into the house, letting the screen door slam behind her.

Daddy grabbed the door handle. "Come back here!"

Me, Pick, and Raynelle had been on the receiving end of Daddy's open hand now and then, but he'd never struck Blissie. I aimed to keep it that way. I squeezed myself between him and the door. "Leave her be, Daddy. Lula means heaven and earth to Blissie."

He raised his hand and I cringed against the screen, waiting for the smack I knew was coming. But he didn't hit me.

"Bah!" he bellowed, and turned away. He let out a string of swear-words and give the washstand a kick that sent it flying into the yard. The pan of rinse water up-ended on the porch, dripping water between the planks and bringing Lonesome out from under with a confused look on his face. That dog slunk away from Daddy's rage quick-like.

As my father weaved down the path towards the creek, spouting language that Pastor Justice would sermonize against, I toted the broken washstand to the garden shed for Pick to mend.

I dried the empty wash pan and hung it on its peg outside the door. Blissie poked out her head and looked around afore she stepped onto the porch, a wet spot on the front of her dress from clutching her doll, her eyes big—and even wetter than her dress.

CHAPTER 11

A FAVOR FOR JANE LOUISE

Jane Louise traipsed up the trail the next morning, calling my name.

I hurried onto the porch to hush her, lest she wake Daddy, who had plenty to sleep off.

"I got a favor to ask of you, Adabel."

"A favor?"

She nodded. "Mr. Putney's nephew come in with the empty coal cars this morning. His name is Chester, and he's handsome as a tree of ripe apples."

"What about Corky Danfield?"

"What about him?"

"I thought you was sweet on Corky is what."

"Corky's good enough as boys go, his daddy being a mine boss and all. But Chester's uncle *owns* the mine. And Chester's not bad to look at neither. A girl could do worse."

My mouth couldn't find words. I cocked my head and give Jane Louise a look that told her jist what I thunk.

She shot me a squinty-eyed stare. "Don't you judge me, Adabel Cutler. You know your own sister snuggles up to Lud Webster for free groceries."

I thunk about last week's white bread and yesterday's dented can of peaches, and shook my head. I plumb didn't understand how either Raynelle or Jane Louise could pretend to like a boy if they really didn't. I know I couldn't.

"Will you come with me to Mr. Putney's office?" Jane Louise asked. "I jist got to meet up with Chester face-to-face afore some other girl catches his eye."

"Why in tarnation would we go to Mr. Putney's office? You goin' sashay in there and say, 'Hey, Mr. Putney, sir, we'd like to meet up with your nephew if'n ya don't mind'? He'll think we're crazy. Jist like I think you are."

"He'll think we got good manners. Mama got holt of some early apples and baked a brown Betty to fetch over as a welcome-to-Smoke-Ridge gift."

"Where'd your mama git apples? And why's she letting ya give food away to a stranger? A stranger whose uncle's got more money than all the rest of Smoke Ridge put together?"

"She knows them are the kind of folks we need to be nicest to. Them're the ones worth having as friends."

I blew out my breath. "Why ya need me to go?"

"It'll look more natural-like if there's two of us. Like we's an official committee or such."

"A committee of two?"

"Please, Adabel. Ya's my best friend, ain't ya?"

Us Cutlers didn't have many friends. Most folks tried to keep their young'uns clear of us. I couldn't afford to rile the only girl in Smoke Ridge who didn't mind being seen with me.

"Wait till I finish my chores," I told her. "I'll meet ya in a' hour."

I scrubbed the floor, thankful for once the house was small.

I swept the porches, front and back, thinking how Jane Louise wanted friends who had money. I didn't have enough pennies to count to one. Why was she friends with me?

CHAPTER 12

THE PAINTING

I pondered how I'd let Jane Louise talk me into this as we stood outside Mr. Putney's office door. The tiny wood building would'a looked smaller'n an outhouse if ya stood it up aside the Putneys' pricey house on Pine View Hill.

Jane Louise waited for me to knock. "*I* cain't knock," she said. "My hands is full of brown Betty. I cain't chance dropping it and wasting good food."

To my thinking, giving it to Chester Putney was already wasting it. But its scent wasn't wasted. The smell of apples and sweetness swaggered up my nose and made my stomach growl.

I took a deep sniff and reckoned I might as well git it over with. I knocked on the wood door.

"Come on in," hollered a voice from inside.

Jane Louise told me with her eyes and the cock of her head to open the door.

"I know," I said. "Your hands is full."

I twisted the knob and pushed open the heavy door, but I stepped back and made Jane Louise go in first, where once again, the tadpole turned into a frog.

"Hey there, Mr. Putney," she said, eyelashes all a-flutter.

I was plumb embarrassed watching Jane Louise act like that to a growed man.

"We come to welcome your nephew to Smoke Ridge," she went on. "Me and my mama baked a brown Betty for him. Is Chester here?" Her eyes looked around the small room, but it didn't take two seconds to see he wasn't. Mr. Putney's desk filled most of the room, and windows shed sunlight across his face and a painting on the wall behind him.

I tried to look interested in that painting to keep from watching Jane Louise make a dang fool of herself. A springtime scene with a bucket of yellow spice bush flowers, it made me recall the bushes that used to bloom along the woods by our old house. I could almost smell their fragrant leaves.

"Sorry, girls," said Mr. Putney, "Chester's fetching papers for me from one of the mine bosses. I'll tell him you came by."

Jane Louise set her wax-paper-covered pan on the only place where the desk wasn't cluttered with stacks of papers. "Tell him this is from Jane Louise Heckathorn. Me and Mama live jist down from Schoolhouse Hill."

She waited for me to introduce myself, but I couldn't peel my eyes off that painting. The bucket of spice bush flowers stood by a fence that trailed away from a cottonwood in full bloom. I could picture the cottonwood branches moving in the breeze, making rustling sounds. And my mind heard other sounds. The creak of a rocking chair. Voices talking. A girl singing. Blissie!

I knew that cottonwood. And that fence. The picture didn't show its rotted places—that fence fell down a few years ago. But the cottonwood was still there, well past its blooming season now. I seen it jist last week. At my old house.

Jane Louise made an impatient sound in her throat, and Mr. Putney stood up and leaned across his desk, looking at me close.

"You're one of the Cutler girls, ain't ya?"

I nodded without a word, my eyes still looking at that cottonwood. Raynelle's voice scolded in my head. *Remember your manners, Adabel.*

"Yes, sir," I answered Mr. Putney.

"Your daddy works for me," he said.

Once my mouth was open, manners fled. I pointed. "The tree in that picture sets outside my old house. Where'd ya git it?"

Jane Louise's mouth opened, too. "Don't be rude, Adabel."

"Adabel?" Mr. Putney said. "So you were named for your mother."

I nodded so hard my eyes blurred. "You knew Mama?"

"I surely did. She painted that picture you're looking at."

"She did? And she give it to you?"

Mr. Putney stammered a mite afore he said, "Not 'give' exactly. We done some bartering for it."

I wondered what kind of bartering, but he didn't say. Besides, the question I wanted answered was the one I seemed to ask ever'body lately. "Do you know why my mama left Smoke Ridge? And where she went?"

Mr. Putney shook his head. "I figured she went to the city to study art. She always wanted to. But I don't know for a fact that's what she did."

"Thank you for your time, Mr. Putney," Jane Louise said. "Be sure to tell Chester that Jane Louise Heckathorn was here. Jane Louise. Jist down from Schoolhouse Hill." She tugged my arm.

"Nice of y'all to stop by," he said.

It was hard to pry my eyes away from Mama's painting, but Jane Louise was fixing to yank my arm clean off.

As soon as we was out the door, Jane Louise looked me square in the face. "Why didn't ya tell me your mama was a painter?"

"I didn't know. Not until now."

"Ain't that funny?" she said.

But it wasn't funny. It was downright discombobulating. On one side, I was happy to know more about Mama. But my other side wanted to know why Mr. Putney knew more about her than I did.

CHAPTER 13

RAYNELLE REMEMBERS

"Raynelle!" I called out in a loud whisper, as I strode through the back door. Loud on account'a Raynelle's back was to me, and a whisper on account'a Daddy's door was closed. That usually meant he was sleeping one off.

A sudsy finger to Raynelle's lips shushed me and told me I was right about Daddy.

I yanked a dish towel from a curtained-off shelf aside the stove and dried the blue-flowered dishes as Raynelle washed.

"Have ya ever seen the painting in Mr. Putney's office?" I asked.

"I cain't recall ever being in his office. How do you know what his office is like?"

"I went there with Jane Louise. She had . . . um, something to drop off for her mama."

"And Jane Louise and her mama are well?" she asked. "It must be hard for 'em since Mr. Heckathorn passed last year."

"They's fine," I snapped. "About the painting. It's a picture of the cottonwood and fence from up at our old house."

"That's nice."

Nice? That's nice? "He said Mama painted it and done bartered it to him. Why ya reckon she done that?"

"A body will do all manner of things to put food on the table when times git lean."

"But that was back afore times got lean," I said.

"I cain't recall a time when they wasn't."

"When we lived in the old house and Daddy worked a full shift at the mine, we never went hungry."

Raynelle's eyes was off remembering things. "No, we wasn't hungry, but Mama always had to keep close watch on our money. Times was never truly good around here."

"But the painting, Raynelle? What about the painting? Mr. Putney said Mama painted it. Do ya recollect Mama painting?

"I do." Raynelle's mouth turned up a tad on the ends. "How Mama loved to paint!" Her eyes stared over my shoulder as if she was seeing things I couldn't. "She used'a spend hours a-setting on the front porch painting flowers and trees and ever'thing in our old yard."

"If Mama spent hours painting, what happened to 'em all?"

"I ain't sure, but I recollect her painting one picture atop another on account'a new canvas was pricey. So it ain't like she had a heap of paintings. But I reckon there might could be a few around here somewhere."

I wanted to tear the house apart to find them paintings, but Raynelle said there was too much work to do. When the dishes was dried and put away, she was quiet. The smile that tugged on the corners of her mouth told me she was remembering happy times—and Mama.

"Raynelle," I said, turning her face to mine. "How come you remember Mama and her paintings, and I don't?"

"You remember. Think on it. We all used'a set there and watch her mix colors together until she come up with jist the right one to match the cornstalks or the sky."

But Raynelle was wrong. I couldn't remember one speck of it. What kind of daughter don't remember her mama?

CHAPTER 14

PICK'S
SHINER

Ever'time I mentioned looking for Mama's paintings, Raynelle reminded me of summer chores that needed doing. Summer days didn't allow time for digging up any more truths or rumors about Mama neither. What I dug up was weeds. Garden work kept me busy—and hot. Sweat seeped down my face, my back, my front, and my legs. Why was weeds so blasted hardy?

As I picked the first ripe tomatoes, thoughts of Mama swirled in my head. If she went to the city to study art, which city did she go to? Charleston? Lexington? Or maybe a la-di-da city like New York or Paris, France? It seemed sensible she wouldn't cart along them old-fashioned dresses from the trunk. She'd want new, stylish clothes from Sears, Roebuck, or Montgomery Ward. Might be that's what she bartered out of Mr. Putney with her painting. Clothes money.

I plumb tired out my memory trying to find a trace of her.

Daddy's Fourth of July celebrating turned into three days of being liquored up and falling down.

Pick showed up at breakfast one morning with a black-and-blue shiner around one eye.

"What happened to you?" I asked.

No answer.

"Was you in a fight?"

He looked over to the door of Daddy's room. "Daddy still sleeping it off?"

I nodded. "Does Daddy know you was in a fight?"

"Wasn't no fight. And Daddy knows."

"Daddy knows?" Just how much did Daddy know? And how come? "Was it Daddy that hit you, Pick?"

"It don't matter who done what. It's over with."

"That don't look like an open-hand smack. Daddy don't use his fists on us."

He looked down at his hands. "Never did afore."

My mouth hung open as I watched Pick wolf down his one-egg breakfast in two bites. His face was as skinny as a plucked chicken's neck.

I slid my plate towards him. "Ya want the rest of mine?"

"You ain't hungry?"

"Not hardly," I said—even though my stomach pined for more.

His fork scraped my egg from the plate right into his mouth. He dropped the dish aside the sink and lit out. I seen him rush through his chores as I pulled weeds and picked bugs off potato plants. My mind wrestled with the thought of Daddy punching Pick. I wanted to punch Daddy, but I took out my anger on weeds and bugs.

Before long, Pick headed off down the hill.

"Where ya going?" I called after him.

He called something back, but it was hard to make out what he said. It sounded like "Nancy." Was Pick sweet on some girl?

As I tried to recollect somebody in Smoke Ridge named Nancy, I pinched ears of corn and looked at the color of their tassels. Some was almost ready. Another few days ought'a do it. Seeing Pick bite into an ear of fresh corn would be worth the battle with watering and weeds.

Yancey! It finally hit me. Pick didn't say "Nancy." He said "Yancey." Teacher Bromley lived down in Yancey over summers when school was out. Likely, Pick was sniffing out more learning. I had hopes Teacher Bromley would fill his stomach as well as his head. And maybe she'd dose his eye.

Pick's shiner faded to a dull red-purple in the next day or so. When I asked why Daddy'd hit him, he shook his head. "Daddy thinks he kin tell me who I got a right to talk to. I'm almost sixteen. I kin talk to anybody I want to."

CHAPTER 15

THE CORN

Pick kept a sizable distance from Daddy except at mealtime. And no words passed betwixt 'em for days. It was a loud kind of quiet that hurt my ears.

They still hadn't said shucks to each other by the day I felt certain I'd be able to find enough ripe ears on the cornstalks for Friday supper. And maybe enough left over for Raynelle to make corn pudd'n on Saturday.

I fetched a basket out to the garden patch, but when my hand reached out, it come back empty. I blinked over and over, not believing what I wasn't seeing. I looked up and down ever' one of them cornstalks that was laden with ears jist yesterday. But there wasn't one single ear of corn. Not one.

"Raynelle!" I hollered, and ran to the house. "Somebody done stole our corn! Ever' bite of it!"

Raynelle hurried out to the back porch, drying her hands on her apron. "Ya got to be wrong. Look again."

Look again? I ain't blind. How could I miss all that corn?

She looked up and down the stalks jist like I done, her face growing more and more distraught. "It cain't be. That corn was s'posed to last us all summer and into fall, with cornmeal for winter baking and hominy to make grits. We need that corn!"

She crawled in the dirt under the stalks, scrabbling around like a mad squirrel, then drew herself up to her knees with shreds of cornhusk clinging in her hair. She sighed. "Even the green ones is gone."

We both eyed Lonesome in one look. Lying by the porch step, he raised up his head afore he trotted out and skittered around us, ready to play.

"Lonesome, what happened?" Raynelle asked, as if she expected that dog could answer.

It would'a took somebody a couple hours or more to pick all that corn and cart it off. Or a bunch of somebodies. What did Lonesome do whilst it was happening?

For a fact, losing that corn was a catastrophe, but another thought pecked in my brain. "Who's goin' tell Daddy?" I asked.

We couldn't let Pick break the news. Not after that shiner. And not sweet little Blissie. That left me or Raynelle.

I watched my sister's face as she traipsed back inside and picked up with her household chores. I never seen that face hang so heavy or look so lost.

I went to the backhouse and set there long past finished what I went to do. I don't usually set there long on account'a the outhouse smell. But I needed to think. Would Daddy take down his twelve-gauge shotgun and set out to find the thief, or vent his anger on the bearer of the news? It was a mine-working day for Daddy, and if he come straight home, he'd still be sober.

When I went back inside, Raynelle leaned on the table, crying into her hands. Strong, capable Raynelle. Crying. She looked up at me, her eyes tinged with red. "How am I goin' feed this family?"

She let out a sob. "How am I goin' tell Daddy?"

"I don't know nothing about how to feed a family," I said, "but I'm the one s'posed to take care of the garden. I'll tell Daddy about the corn gone missing."

CHAPTER 16

TELLING DADDY

Daddy come home late, and Raynelle had moved the baked-bean casserole from the oven to the warming shelf above the stove.

As he come through the door, a layer of coal dust coating his mining clothes and beard, he walked straight and didn't seem as drunk as sometimes. The lines around his eyes were mapped in black, and words with a hint of slur sailed from his mouth on waves of moonshine breath. Telling him wasn't goin' be easy.

Raynelle's hands shook as she carried the baked beans to the supper table. Me and her exchanged worried glances.

We hadn't told Pick about the corn yet. The color under his eye was tinged with yellow, a sign it was near healed, but I reckoned he still had the kind of bruises that didn't show.

I waited until Daddy'd eaten enough casserole to take the edge off'n his hunger. I reached deep inside me in search of a steady voice—not a common thing for me. "Daddy," I said. "We's been preyed on by a thief. The corn's been stole. All of it."

"What?" It wasn't Daddy who bellowed the word. It was Pick. I was ready for Daddy's temper, but Pick's tone caught me by surprise. "What happened?"

Daddy's eyes looked up slow, and he finished spooning in a bite of beans. He chewed a mite afore he spoke. "Lonesome didn't bark? Didn't run the stranger off afore he stole?"

"Me and Raynelle didn't hear nothing," I said.

"Me neither," Blissie added.

Daddy squinted at each of us in turn. "You wasn't off lollygagging instead of minding the house?"

"No, Daddy," Raynelle said. "I been here all day. Yesterday, too."

His squint lingered on Raynelle. "Lud Webster didn't come around, turning your head and distracting ya from your chores?"

Raynelle blushed. "I ain't seen Lud all week."

"It's true, Daddy," I put in.

Daddy ran his black fingernails through his hair and shook his head. "Dang shame," he said, just *said*, not yelled or cussed or kicked things. "Lonesome had a job to do. I'm right disappointed in that dog."

I set there stunned, wondering if this was the *calm before the storm* we hear tell about. I braced myself for the thunder.

Pick had gone quiet, and I could almost see his brain talking things out with itself. His eyes shifted from me to Daddy to Raynelle and back to Daddy again.

"I don't know how we's goin' git through a year without a corn crop," Raynelle said. "What are we goin' eat?"

"Yeah, Daddy," Pick said. "What're we goin' eat?"

I didn't say nothing. I'd always been skinny, so it didn't show on me like it done on Pick, but how long could we keep on without ample food on the table?

"Beans is still cheap," Daddy said. "We'll git by."

I couldn't believe how unruffled Daddy was. It seemed like somebody else's daddy was a-setting at our table.

Pick stood up, even though beans was still on his plate. He looked down at Daddy. "Now why do you s'pose Lonesome didn't bark, Daddy?" His tone carried suspicion.

Hush up, Pick, I said inside my head. *Don't push him.*

Daddy's voice rose a speck or two. "How the devil should I know?"

"I reckon," Pick said even-like, "Lonesome didn't run off no stranger on account of there wasn't no stranger. Most likely, the thief had a smell Lonesome knew."

"Could'a been a neighbor, I s'pose," Daddy said.

Pick's even tone raised up a heap, and he crossed his arms over his chest. "Could'a been somebody from this very house."

My fork dropped on my plate with a *clink*.

Daddy stood up with a riled look I never seen afore without him being drunker'n Grant's horse. "Surely ya ain't saying one of your sisters done this."

Pick didn't budge, didn't take his eyes off Daddy. "No, Daddy, I ain't."

Daddy stepped around the table and stood with his nose just inches away from Pick's. "Then jist what *are* you saying?"

Pick dropped his hands to his sides, and I seen him curl 'em into fists. He didn't back away from Daddy. "What I'm saying is . . ." He spat the words right in Daddy's face. "If a moonshiner wants corn to make mash, he might trade moonshine for corn. And nobody would take food out'a his family's mouths to trade for 'shine except . . ." His next words come out slow and loud, and one finger rose to Daddy's chest, giving it a sturdy poke with each word. "A lousy. Consarn. No-account. Stinking. Drunk."

Daddy flinched a hardly noticeable little flinch. "Take it back," he ordered.

Pick's voice thundered as strong as Daddy's. "You denying it?"

"One more chance to take it back." Daddy's voice bounced off the wall. "Last chance."

Pick stayed silent.

Daddy stepped back one step afore his fist swung out and caught Pick's nose. Blood squirted out, and Pick's fist hit back. Us girls jumped from our chairs as Daddy threw another punch.

"Cut it out, Daddy! Pick, stop!" I screamed. "Raynelle! Make 'em stop!"

Daddy shoved Pick into the table, and baked-bean casserole slid towards the edge. Raynelle snatched up the pan quick, but two of the blue-flowered plates slid to the floor with a crash.

Pick recoiled and tore at Daddy, pummeling him with punch after punch. Daddy fought back and the two of 'em scuffled on the floor like rabid dogs, fists and red hair a-flying in a cloud of coal dust.

Blissie grabbed Lula and scurried to shelter beside the old trunk, tears streaming down her face.

When the only sound was loud breathing, Pick was sprawled out on the floor, Daddy straddling his chest. Daddy took in gulps of air and demanded again, "Take it back."

Pick gasped betwixt ragged breaths. "Soon's you tell me why Lonesome didn't bark."

Daddy didn't answer. Jist got to his feet and slammed out the screen door.

CHAPTER 17

AFTER THE FIGHT

My hands shaking considerable, I righted a chair that had gone sidewise during the scrap and helped Pick to sit. His face was bloodied, and Raynelle brought a cloth and pan of water to clean him up. The more she cleaned, the worse he looked. A flap of skin hung down from his cheek and his nose was swole up like a tomato. He winced ever'time Raynelle dabbed at his face.

"Ya need stitched up, Pick," I said. "Ya want I should fetch the doctor from down in Evarts?"

"No."

"But—"

"I said no." His voice was firm.

Raynelle bandaged him up best she could. "You should sleep in our room tonight," she suggested. Daddy slept in one bedroom and us girls shared t'other, but Pick's bed was in a corner of the main room. "You don't want to be out here when Daddy comes home. Like as not, he's nursing his own wounds with liquor."

Pick got to his feet, pain etched across his face as he moved. "I ain't staying here tonight."

"But, Pick . . ."

"I'll go down to Shovel's. His mama'll let me sleep there."

We tried to stop him, but Pick scooted out the door.

Norris and his family lived just three company-owned shanties down from us, so I reckoned it wasn't a bad idea. But letting other folks know our business didn't seem wise neither.

Raynelle calmed Blissie down and sent her and Lula to bed, afore me and her set to cleaning up the mess. Baked beans was ever'where. On the table, chairs, floor. Even on Mama's trunk.

Raynelle didn't speak. Me neither. We had to be doing the same thinking. *Was Pick right? Could Daddy'a done this to us?* A man who done what Daddy jist done to Pick might do anything.

A sound from outside made us jump, until we realized it was Lonesome settling in under the back porch for the night.

We was well-past settled ourselves when we heard Daddy come home. I reached through the dark for Raynelle's hand, and she give mine a squeeze.

Next morning, Daddy was a-setting at the table, bruised considerable with a swole lip and dried blood caked in his beard, but no trace of a morning-after look to him. "Pick around?"

"No, Daddy," I said, hoping he wouldn't ask where Pick was.

He didn't. The only sounds was the *clink* of dishes as I set the table and the scrape of Raynelle's wood spoon against the pan as she stirred up grits. I noticed the empty hominy crock. Last grits of the year. And without corn, none next year neither.

Not until Raynelle plunked the pan on the table, and me and her set down, did Daddy talk. "Weren't right what I done last night. I hope you girls know I never meant to hurt your brother."

Daddy being penitent was a strange thing. It give me courage to say, "Ya ought'a say that to Pick."

Daddy ignored my words. "I'm right sorry I got so riled. But what he done wasn't right neither."

I knew not to open my mouth, but I couldn't help it. I had to know. "You mean he was wrong to hit ya or he was wrong about you taking our corn?"

"You girls think I'd do such a thing?"

Blissie shook her head. "No, Daddy."

Raynelle's head-shake was small and wordless.

Daddy looked at me. "Adabel?"

I breathed in deep and let it out slow, whilst in my head I pictured the way Daddy beat on Pick. When Daddy wasn't even slop-faced drunk. I looked him square in the eye afore I said, "I ain't sure what to think, Daddy."

He banged his hands hard on the table, and I froze, thinking he might hit me. Or punch me like he done Pick. I looked down at the table and waited for his words—or his hand.

But he picked up his fork and ate his breakfast. Like a daddy who wasn't ours.

CHAPTER 18

PICK
REMEMBERS

Pick stayed gone for three days—until Daddy's next mine shift come around. Mine work commenced early in the morning, even though mines was dark as night anytime. Carbide lanterns on the miners' hats allowed them to see as they toiled deep underground.

I was gathering up breakfast dishes when Pick slipped in and plunked a bucket of blackberries on the table. His face was similar colors to the berries, and a scrap of gauze was taped over his cut cheek.

"Me and Shovel went berry-picking first thing this morning," he said.

"Ya want breakfast?" Raynelle asked.

"Shovel's mama cooked. And I done stuffed myself on berries. I got three days of chores to catch up on." He scooted outside, letting the screen door bang behind him.

Raynelle washed the blackberries in cold water, and I reached in for one. Biting into its sweetness made me crave more, but Raynelle's look told me to keep my hands off.

"Where ya reckon he found 'em?" she said.

"Don't know, but unless the sheriff comes sniffing around looking for stole berries, I reckon we ought'a jist enjoy 'em and don't ask no questions."

Raynelle smiled. "We'll have some at noontime, and I kin put up a few jars for winter. Won't blackberry jam taste good at Christmas time?"

After my chores, I found Pick on the back porch fixing the busted washstand Daddy kicked the day of Lula's bath. I saw the way he avoided wiping sweat from his bruised, tore-up face.

"You don't need to fix that now," I said.

He pulled a nail from betwixt his lips to say, "I want things took care of afore I leave."

"Ya going back to Norris's?"

"I cain't stay here with that man no more," he said, and took to pounding in the nail, letting the hammer's noise drown out anything I might say.

I waited until the pounding quit. "No matter what he done, that man is our daddy. With no mama, he's all we got. He come home the morning after the fight to say sorry, but you wasn't home to hear it." I couldn't believe I was defending Daddy.

Pick grunted and started pounding again.

I leaned against the porch rail, running my fingers along its rough wood, whilst Pick stood the washstand on its four legs, two old and two new. He rocked it to see if it wobbled, turned it on end, and took sandpaper to its feet.

"Things was quiet with you gone," I said.

"Quiet ain't bad," he said. "After the ruckus t'other night, quiet must'a been right nice."

"Quiet feels kind'a . . . kind'a empty," I said. And there was already too much empty. "Pick, do you recollect Mama?"

"'Course I do. A body don't forgit his mama."

Don't they? What's wrong with me? "What do you remember about her?"

He paused for a speck, staring out towards the treetops. "She hummed whilst she did housework. 'Turkey in the Straw' for dusting and sweeping, 'Buffalo Gals' for cooking, and church hymns for washing dishes."

For a few seconds, I thunk I heard Mama's humming in my head, but it weren't Mama at all. Raynelle always sang under her breath whilst she cooked. Raynelle's voice was what I remembered.

"And when she ironed, she recited words from a poem," Pick went on. "A poem about a swing. She'd recite it whilst she ironed each shirt, finishing up on the last line. *Up in the air and down.* She'd lift up her iron and plunk it back on the stove in time to the words."

Up in the air and down. I recollected hearing them words, but it weren't Mama's voice I heard. It was a male voice.

"I read to Mama from my school books," Pick said. "When I come to a word I didn't know, she'd say, 'Jist sound it out.'"

"You always liked reading, didn't ya?" I said.

"Still do. After a while I knew Mama made me sound out words on account'a she didn't know 'em. Mama couldn't read."

"She couldn't?" I felt close to Mama in that moment, even if I couldn't remember her. I knew all my letters, but the words they spelled out always give me fits.

"Don't ya remember when Miz Webster give her the receipt for applesauce cake, and Mama made Raynelle read it to her?"

"No. I don't. I don't remember Miz Webster." My voice went

high and wobbly. "And I don't remember Mama at all."

His eyes got big and stared at me as though my mind had up and left me. "You truly don't?"

Tears flooded my eyes. "Why cain't I remember her, Pick? You do and you're jist two years older'n me."

He put his arm around my shoulders and dried my eyes on the hem of his shirt.

"I don't even remember Daddy telling us she left," I said with a sniff. "I just recollect you and Raynelle saying he did."

"Maybe it's for the best," Pick said. "You cain't miss a body you don't remember."

But he was wrong. So wrong. At least he had his memories. I had nothing. As though I'd never had a mama.

CHAPTER 19

PICK'S THINKING

"How long ya staying with Norris?" I asked.

"Ain't going there." Pick looked off into the distance. "I'm leaving for good."

No! I grabbed his arm. "What? Why?"

"Ya know why. Ya seen what Daddy done. And he wasn't far gone at the time. What's he goin' do next time he's drunk?"

"Ya got him riled, Pick. Ya laid blame ya don't know he deserves."

"And why do *you* think Lonesome didn't bark? Lonesome would'a bit a chunk of flesh from a no-good thief."

"I ain't sure what to think."

"Well, I'm sure. The no-good thief was our daddy. Daddy's a drunk, Adabel. Nothing's as important to him as his next drink. Not even us."

"You cain't mean that."

"Remember back when he sent us away? What kind of man sends away his own young'uns? I was only eight years old, and it hurt considerable to think he didn't want us no more. 'Specially after we jist lost Mama."

Sent us away? When Pick was eight? I would'a been six, but I didn't remember no such of a thing.

"He never come around," Pick said. "Never come ta see how I was doing. And jist when I got used to living with Shovel, Daddy come and hauled me back home. He should'a jist left me there."

My mind couldn't find a lick of sense in his words. "Sent us away? What you talking about, Pick?"

"Don't ya remember? When Mama first left, Daddy shunted us young'uns off. Me to Shovel's. Raynelle and Blissie to Granny Cutler's. And you . . . I cain't recall who he give you to. Was it Jane Louise's mama?"

"I don't recollect none of that. I only remember living in the old house with y'all. Till we moved here last year. It's always been us. You, me, Raynelle, Blissie, and Daddy."

"Ya's lucky not to remember ever'thing. Some things is best forgot."

"Ya's wrong, Pick." A mind full of empty places was worse'n the awfulest memories a body could have.

Pick stood the washstand up and brushed the shavings off it. He slid the sandpaper into its paper sleeve and tucked it in the toolbox.

"I'll put this away and git my things," he said.

I traipsed behind him to the shed. "Please don't leave, Pick."

"Daddy done left me no choice," he said over his shoulder. "And food'll stretch further with one less stomach at the table."

"But where will you go?"

"I ain't for sure yet, but I have me some thoughts on it." He set the washstand in a corner of the shed and slid the toolbox on a shelf.

"What thoughts?" I asked.

"Better ya don't know," he said, hanging the hammer on its peg on the shed wall. "I don't want ya gitting some mule-brained idea to come looking for me."

"Don't go." I was truly begging. "We's a family. We belong together." The hammer hung in a row of other tools Pick used on account'a Daddy was often too drunk to handle 'em. The axe he used for splitting wood. The spade he turned the earth with for spring planting. Rake. Hoe. Saw. Shears. Coal shovel. A pick. "What'll we do with you gone?"

He avoided my eyes, as if closing the shed door took serious thinking. "Raynelle can handle things."

"But she talks like she's goin' marry Luddy Webster. What if she up and does? And moves in with him somewheres? She's closest to a mama we got. I cain't take care of Blissie and the house on my own. I jist cain't."

He stood still, a shadow coming over his face like a cloud crossing the sun. But it wasn't a real shadow, just a bad-feeling look. "Why ya reckon we got no mama?" he asked.

"She run off. Ain't that what Daddy said?"

He nodded. "That's what he said, but why would she do such a thing?"

"I don't know, Pick. I wish to God in Heaven I did."

He looked down at his hands. "I done me some thinking these last few days."

"Thinking about Mama?"

"Thinking about Daddy." He raised his eyes slowly and locked on mine. "You seen how he is when he's drunk. What if he tore into Mama like he tore into me t'other night?"

"Are ya jist supposing or do ya recollect Daddy beating Mama?"

"He beats the rest of us. Wouldn't surprise me a lick if'n he hit her too hard once too often." His voice dropped to a whisper. "Might be he buried her body up by our old house."

"You don't mean that!" I shouted, afore dropping my own voice to a whisper. "Daddy could never kill Mama. Or anybody."

"The Mama I remember wouldn't have jist up and left without hugging and kissing us. She wouldn'ta done that. She loved us!"

"If she loved us so much, how come I cain't even remember her? Mr. Putney thinks she went to the city to study art."

"Mr. Putney don't know nothing. And you'd remember Mama if ya thunk on it hard enough. She was a good and loving mama. Daddy gits the devil inside him whenever he drinks. You know that."

"I don't care what you say. I'll never believe Daddy kilt Mama." But even as the words left my mouth, doubts jumped into my head. Being dead would explain why she didn't take her dresses. Or why nobody'd heard from her in seven years.

No! I couldn't believe that!

CHAPTER 20

THE EMPTY PLACE

Raynelle jist shook her head when I told her Pick left. She already knew. But I didn't think he'd said anything to her about Daddy killing Mama. It was hard for me to even think them words.

"Why didn't ya stop him?" I screeched.

"How was I s'posed to do that? Lock him in his room? He don't even have a room of his own. Likely he'll wear out his anger and wander home sooner or later."

I wished I could believe that. But she hadn't seen the determined look on his face when he said, "I'm leaving for good." For good! *For good* meant never coming back. And she hadn't seen the shadowed look that told me what he thunk Daddy might'a done. But he was wrong! I had to prove it. The onliest way to prove it was to find out where Mama went. Somebody had to know.

But I had no time for asking folks questions. With Pick gone, the rest of us had to take on his chores as well as our own, trying to fill the new empty place in our family. An empty, aching hole of a place. A place only Pick could fill.

"When's Pick coming home?" Blissie asked. She asked the question ever' day. Day after day after day. And I had no answer for her. I didn't have the gumption to tell her he'd never come home. Ever. It was hard for me to convince myself it was true.

When she asked, I found chores for her to do. She scattered scraps for the chickens and scared up dead branches from down in the woods to feed the cook stove. Raynelle did most all her cooking with wood now to save coal money for winter. How odd to scrimp for coal when Daddy worked inside tunnels of it two days a week.

"With no corn, I'll be needing to buy cornmeal or flour down to the store," Raynelle said. "I got to watch ever' penny."

She made hot suppers and served cold leftovers for breakfasts and lunches. Not building a fire in the morning kept the house cooler, but cold bean soup day after day made going hungry almost appealing.

With no corn, I didn't have to water the corn patch no more. We had cabbage, tomatoes, and green beans. I hankered after the squeak of green beans betwixt my teeth, but Raynelle wanted to save most of 'em to dry and string for winter eating.

No matter how lean the meal was, Daddy never complained. He fidgeted some when his plate was empty, but not a word of gripe. I wondered if that was on account'a he had a stomach full'a blame from trading away our corn.

He barely spoke, his mind always seeming to be somewhere else. I didn't know which scared me more. Bellowing, cussing, fighting-mad Daddy? Or the Daddy who didn't say nothing a'tall?

CHAPTER 21

A FEW MINUTES OF HOPE

On the morning after an all-night August rainstorm, the garden didn't need watering, and the weeds pulled up easy. My chores finished early, I skittered away right after helping with lunch dishes, afore Raynelle could find more for me to do.

I traipsed up to the old house. No moonshine jars set behind the *For Sale or Rent* sign.

I walked clean around the house, turning over rocks and looking close at ever' crack in the foundation. But all I found was bugs and weeds and a foundation that hadn't been looked after for a spell. No place a body might be buried. But Mama was gone seven years. It wasn't like there'd be fresh-turned earth to mark a grave. *And Daddy didn't kill Mama. He just plain didn't.* And didn't Raynelle say Daddy wanted Mama's dresses kept nice just in case? He wouldn'ta worried on that if he knew Mama was dead.

Sitting on the porch step, I tried to conjure thoughts of Mama into my head. I recollected days spent in this house, but not Mama. Raynelle cooked meals in a kitchen that was separate from the sitting room, and Pick had his own room to sleep in. A house so much bigger'n a miner's shanty.

I turned and looked at the house. Daddy'd been a miner then, jist like now. Only he'd worked a full week, instead of jist two days. While Mr. Shortwell and most other miners lived in shanties, we'd lived in this big five-room house. On account'a Granddaddy Cutler selling it cheap to Daddy. But now we lived like most miners. In shanties so close together you could almost hear your neighbor's ever' cough. Shanties owned by Mr. Putney.

You could pile all the things us Cutlers owned onto this porch, and have room left over. I plumb hated being poor.

I meandered through the old vegetable patch, a patch five times bigger'n what we had now. I remembered it ripe with good things to eat instead of brown and dead and full of weeds.

A green lighter than weeds caught my eye, and I looked closer. A green tomato! Two of 'em! On a plant that'd pushed up through the soil on its own. Like as not, one of our old tomatoes fell to the ground or got nibbled on by rabbits or deer, and its seeds took root. It'd struggled through with no one to take care of it, and now it had tomatoes a-growing on it.

It didn't crave water on account'a last night's rain. I'd have to bring a shovel to dig it up and take it to plant in our new garden, where I could make sure it got watered ever' day.

One tomato plant wouldn't make a whole heap of difference towards feeding us, but I felt myself smile as I strolled down to the hemlock grove. Sitting in the cool, shadowy dark betwixt the trees, I tried to convince myself that us Cutlers—like that tomato plant—would git through these Hard Times.

But we wasn't the same Cutlers no more. I knew Blissie would come home from school and ask, "When's Pick coming home?"

I couldn't answer her question or none of my own. And I

couldn't bring Pick home the way I could a tomato plant.

My fingers sifted through hemlock needles and my mind sifted through questions. I was no closer to an answer about where Mama went than I'd been in June. Did Daddy trade our corn away to some moonshiner? Did he truly send us young'uns away like Pick said? Why would he do that? And why couldn't I remember? All them lost memories confounded me more than ever. And the hardest question to stew over: Where did Pick go?

Hemlock branches leaned together. Touching one another. Close. Like a family had ought'a be. A breeze stirred last year's dry needles along the ground and made whispering sounds. A sound that reminded me of secrets being kept. Shutting me out. I got up and left the hemlock grove behind. The few minutes of hope planted in me by tomato seeds had dried up and blew away on a breeze.

CHAPTER 22

LIKE OLD DOGS

My mind was so full of questions it didn't pay attention to where my feet was taking me. I ended up at the cemetery that set in a pocket between the hills.

Grass grew tall around the gravestones, but I been there afore and knew where our kin was. Mamaw and Papaw Pickens, Mama's folks, shared a stone. I didn't remember neither one of 'em. They'd been gone a long time.

Granny and Granddaddy Cutler had separate stones. Daddy used'a put flowers on his mama's grave on her birthday ever' year. I recall Daddy's mama jist a speck. She had tight curls dangling by each ear. It felt good to remember *somebody*. Pick said Daddy sent Raynelle and Blissie to stay with Granny Cutler after Mama left. Mama left in 1925. Granny's marker said 1927. Sometime during them two years, ever'thing I knew fell right out'a my head.

If Daddy'd sent us away, why didn't I recollect that? Pick thunk I stayed with Jane Louise. I didn't recall no such a thing.

I quit my lollygagging and sent my feet forward with a purpose. They hurried down the muddy street of Smoke Ridge, past the company stores, blacksmith shop, and Mr. Putney's office, on past the school house, and down the hill to Jane Louise's.

The muggy August air seemed to hang in the holler like a bucket of sweat, dousing me as I come down the hill.

And noise from the mine near-about knocked me off my feet. The mine entry was over the next rise, and all I could see was the top of the tipple where it bent like a knuckle. Full mine cars was hauled up the tipple's tracks with a *ratchety-ratchety* sound, reached the knuckle, tipped, and dumped coal over its edge. Unseen train cars waited on tracks below, and the rattle and bang of coal tumbling into them sounded like a hammer pounding iron.

The noise didn't seem to bother Jane Louise's mama, who set on her porch peeling a potato, the peel hanging in one long strip. The door of the one-room shack was propped open with a rock, but sunshine didn't reach its dark innards.

I'd forgot how tiny the Heckathorn place was. Jane Louise and her mama had moved there after her daddy got kilt down in Evarts over a year ago. Caught in the middle of a fight betwixt angry miners and sheriff's deputies.

"Hey, Miz Heckathorn," I called out. "Is Jane Louise home?"

"No, she ain't, Adabel. She went for a walk with Chester Putney." *Chester Putney? So Jane Louise's plan with the brown Betty worked.* I wondered if Corky Danfield knew she was keeping company with somebody else.

I stood quiet for a moment, watching that potato peel git longer, reaching almost to the porch's floor planks. "Miz Heckathorn, ma'am, when you lived in your old house, did I ever stay there with ya? Back when my mama first left?"

She let the peel drop to the floor and put the peeled potato in a pan. She rubbed the back of the knife blade against her cheek whilst she was thinking. "I don't recall nothing like that. Nothing a'tall."

"But ya recollect Mama leaving?"

"I jist recollect how broke-hearted your daddy was. He loved your mama deep."

It was hard to think of Daddy loving anyone *deep*. I wish Pick could'a heard her say that.

"Mama didn't tell ya she was goin' leave, ma'am? Do ya know what made her go?"

"She never said nothing to me, but some folks thunk your mama was like her mama, and she done left to . . ." Miz Heckathorn picked up another potato to peel without finishing her sentence.

"Left to what? How was Mama like Mamaw Pickens?"

Her knife stopped, and she looked up at me, a bit of a blush creeping across her cheeks. "I ain't quite sure how to explain it," she said. "Ya's a mite young."

"Could ya try?" I asked, barely breathing, waiting, giving her time to think. "I'm older'n I look. Thirteen now."

Her knife commenced to cutting again, and her eyes didn't leave the potato. "Back in them days, Jeff Pickens—yer papaw— was like an old dog," she said, as the strip of peel grew longer. "Jist an old dog a-setting on the porch waiting for his master to open the door and let him in. But your mamaw was more of a frisky dog, running the yard a-chasing squirrels."

"Chasing squirrels?"

She cocked her head sidewise and opened her eyes wide, watching me with a waiting look.

Her meaning finally caught hold. "Glory be!" I said, my own blush spreading up me. "My mamaw? A frisky dog?"

She nodded. "Practically afore the last shovel of dirt was throwed on your papaw's grave, Leona Pickens lit out for parts unknown. Folks said she took up with some feller who had a bit of money to spend on her."

Lit out for parts unknown? But Mamaw Pickens was buried right by her husband's side beneath the same stone. Like two old dogs. I had jist seen it. Hadn't I?

CHAPTER 23

CLEAR EYES

I wanted to go back to the cemetery and take another look at Mamaw Pickens's grave, but the mine whistle blew. I knew I had to git home afore Daddy. My skinny legs scampered up Schoolhouse Hill and past the stores. Folks stared as I scurried by, but I didn't take time to say howdy or nothing.

Over the board that straddled the creek. Up the hill through the woods. I come to the back of our shanty trying to catch my breath. Lonesome looked up as if to say, *Ya's in a heap'a trouble, Adabel.*

Not as much as I'd be if'n Daddy was home, my mind said back.

"Adabel, where'd ya run off to?" Raynelle said from the stove. "Daddy'll be home soon, and supper ain't ready yet. Stir this soup whilst I mash these taters. And fetch Blissie to set the table."

"Taters? Our taters is ready?"

"Not yet, but Lud brung me some that had bad spots on 'em. I cut off the spots afore I boiled 'em."

Blissie answered my yell. Soon as she showed up, dragging Lula by one arm, I stirred the soup. I stared at beans going round and round in the pot, the tired smell of bean soup insulting my nose. Mashed taters would be a tasty change.

I thought back to Miz Heckathorn peeling potatoes. I didn't see no bad spots on hers. How come she had better potatoes than we had? I recollected being surprised when Jane Louise said her mama "got holt of some early apples" to bake a brown Betty for Chester Putney. Since when did the Heckathorns live better'n us?

It confounded me that Pick wasn't here so's I could tell him what Miz Heckathorn said about Daddy loving Mama deep. And that I didn't stay with the Heckathorns after Mama left. He'd been wrong about that. And I was sure he was wrong about other things.

"Raynelle," I said. "Do ya recollect Daddy sending us young'uns away after Mama left? Pick said he stayed with Norris and you and Blissie stayed with Granny Cutler."

Raynelle quit mashing potatoes. "I reckoned Daddy sent me there so's Granny could teach me to cook and sew, afore I come home to keep house." She measured salt in her hand, something she must'a learned from Granny, and sprinkled it in the taters.

"Couldn't Granny move in with us and done it herself? We lived in the big house back then."

"Caring for Granddaddy afore he died wore Granny down to a cinder. She was plumb tired ever' day jist teaching me to keep house and look after Blissie. She wasn't up to taking care of a young'un no more."

"You and Blissie was there, and Pick was with Norris. He said I prob'ly stayed with Jane Louise, but Miz Heckathorn says I didn't. Where was I?" Them words screeched a mite.

"Don't *you* remember where ya stayed?"

"No, I cain't remember nothing." My voice broke and tears filled my eyes. I blinked them away and breathed a ragged breath. I reckoned nobody'd notice a tear or two in the soup.

"I don't remember neither," Blissie said.

"But you was jist a baby." My voice raised up. "You ain't s'posed to remember."

"It was a long time ago," Raynelle said. "It don't matter."

But it did matter. It mattered to me!

"We got other things to think on right now," she said. "Keep stirring. Daddy'll be here in a minute."

And in a minute, Daddy showed up. Sober. Again. I tried to count how many days it'd been since I seen him drunk. And it hit me. He hadn't had a drink since the fight with Pick.

I thought back to suppers where I seen him with the shakes and fidgets, and thunk he was jist hungry. And nights I heard him pace the floor. Or thrash around in his bed. It'd been the D.T.'s that come on from lack of drink. Daddy'd quit drinking! I wanted to tell Pick. *Daddy quit drinking, Pick. You kin come home. We kin be a family again.*

Watching Daddy's eyes as he spooned bean soup and mashed taters into his mouth made me smile. They were clear eyes. Sober eyes.

But Pick was a sore spot inside me. I missed him and craved to talk to him, but an anger abided there, too. *Dang you, Pick! Why'd ya have to leave?*

CHAPTER 24

CORKY

Raynelle kept a close eye on me the next day.

"Don't be a-skittering away again," she said. "Ya got chores to do."

Daddy didn't work a mine shift that day, so his eyes, clear and sober, kept watch on me, too. I couldn't slip away to the cemetery to look at Mamaw Pickens's gravestone. And I couldn't go looking for Pick. Not that I could do that anyhow.

Having Daddy sober give us extra hands to do Pick's work, but the work didn't do nothing to calm the feelings churning inside of me. How could one heart have room for such anger and an aching loss at the same time?

I washed the windows in the back of our shanty and worked my way around to the front ones. We didn't use our front door much, though we propped it open in warm weather to let air flow through from front door to back. The back porch was closest to the trail towards Smoke Ridge. Taking the road from out front was the long way around.

Even this far from the mine, coal dust carried and clung to windowpanes and turned my wash water black as soot. Taking my anger out on the dirt, I rinsed the rag for the hundredth time. And I heard my name.

82

"Adabel," a boy's voice said. "Kin I talk to ya for a minute?"

I turned to see Corky Danfield. "If'n ya kin talk whilst I work," I said.

"I'll help ya." He took the wet rag from me and washed the window I'd just finished. I couldn't believe the rag got blacker still.

"You seen Jane Louise lately?" he asked.

I tried to recollect when I last seen her. I hadn't seen her yesterday when I talked to her mama. I knew I hadn't told her about Daddy's fight with Pick or that Pick done left. Not that I'da told her about the fight anyhow. As for Pick's leaving, that was the kind of thing that got around fast in Smoke Ridge.

I thunk back to the day we took the brown Betty to Mr. Putney's office. The day I seen Mama's painting there. More'n a month ago.

"No, Corky, I reckon I ain't."

"Johnny Loomis says she's been keeping company with Mr. Putney's nephew. You know anything about that?"

How do you tell a boy that his girl decided not to be his girl no more? That she done caught herself a bigger fish? I didn't want to hurt his feelings none.

"How would I know what she's of a mind to do?" I said. "She ain't been around for more'n a month."

"I reckon she thinks she kin do better'n me," he said, resentment in his voice and hurt on his face.

I knew he was right, but I couldn't say so. "Jane Louise ain't like that," I lied.

"Sure she is. All girls is like that. Look at your sister. She friendlies up to Lud Webster for dented cans and day-olds."

I jerked the rag out'a his hand. "That ain't so! Git on out'a here afore I tell my daddy what you jist said."

His face went scared for a second, like maybe he'd heard what

83

Daddy was capable of. He turned to walk down the dusty road, but stopped. He come up close to me, close enough to touch me. I shrank back against the shanty wall as he whispered in my ear.

"If *you* ever want to friendly up to a mine boss's son, ya know where to find me." Afore I could stop him, he planted a kiss on my cheek and sauntered off, looking back over his shoulder to grin like a dang fool.

I swiped that dirty black rag across my cheek. "Never!" I yelled after him. "Never in a hundred years!"

CHAPTER 25

NORRIS

A few days later, I told Raynelle about the tomato plant up at the old house, so she let me off from my chores to dig it up.

Of course, afore I even went to the old vegetable patch, I headed up to the cemetery to check Mamaw Pickens's grave.

Walking along the cemetery road, carrying a bucket and shovel, I heard footsteps behind me. I spun around to see Norris Shortwell.

"Hey, Norris, ya scared me a mite. I thunk ya might be Corky Danfield."

"Why'd ya be scared of Corky?"

"He ain't too happy that Jane Louise Heckathorn took up with Chester Putney, and since Jane Louise and me used to be friends, he ain't too happy with me neither."

"What ya mean you and Jane Louise '*used* to be friends'?"

"Jane Louise don't come around no more."

"Oh," he said with a knowing nod.

"She talks like folks with money is the best kind of friends for her, but she was friends with me even though I never had none. I don't know what changed her. Or why she was friends with me in the first place."

"Don't ya?" He squinted at me.

I squinted back. "What ain't ya telling me?"

"It ain't easy knowing that folks is nice on account'a they want something you got."

"But I ain't never had nothing for nobody to want."

"Not no more. But ya *did* have what Jane Louise wanted."

"You don't make no sense, Norris."

"Jane Louise might'a kept company with Corky and Chester for what they has. But the boy she liked deep down in her heart was your brother. Being friends with you put her closer to Pick."

My mouth flew open. "Oh! So now that Pick's gone, she don't need to be my friend no more." I waited for tears, but there wasn't none. I reckon losing a body who was jist using me wasn't a deep hurt like losing a brother.

"Somewheres inside I knew me and Jane Louise wasn't true friends, but I plumb didn't know why. You answered a question that pecked in my brain, Norris. Though I confess it don't feel so good knowing I ain't got no friends no more."

He smiled. "Ya still got me. We's friends, ain't we?"

"I reckon, but jist friends. Ya ain't goin' kiss me or nothing, are ya?"

His smile stretched into a grin. "Not unless ya want me to."

I glared at him. "Why is boys such lugheads?"

"It's girls what make us that way," he said. "You's the one brung up kissing, not me."

We stood in an awkward silence for a minute, him looking like he had more to say. "Ya know I'm doing errands for Mr. Putney," he finally said. "He lets me drive his truck sometimes."

"That's nice, Norris," I said, afore the silence fell betwixt us again. It was strange seeing him so wordless.

86

He broke the quiet by asking, "Where ya headed with that shovel?"

"The cemetery."

"Digging up loved ones or strangers?" he said with a laugh.

I smiled. "Jist digging up truth."

"Speaking of truth, I plumb forgot to tell ya something Pick said."

"You heard from Pick?" A seed of hope dropped into my mind.

"Something he said *afore* he left. He wanted ya to know that he said some things to ya back then, things about your daddy, things said in anger. But they was all bunk. Ya shouldn't believe 'em."

"I knew it! I knew that Daddy . . ." I didn't say more, not knowing if Pick told Norris what them things he said to me was. I didn't reckon Pick would go around telling folks he thunk Daddy kilt Mama, but Norris wasn't jist folks. Him and Pick was true friends, not like me and Jane Louise.

"Thanks for telling me, Norris."

"Ya want I should go to the cemetery with ya?"

I shook my head.

He seemed reluctant to go, but eventually he headed one way whilst I headed t'other.

I turned and watched him, seen the way his feet shuffled through the dirt like he was dragging something heavy behind him. He was Shovel with no Pick, and he must'a hurt considerable. I wasn't the only one with an empty place on account of my brother.

CHAPTER 26

THE CEMETERY

I hadn't truly believed Pick when he said what he'd said, but I felt a heap relieved knowing he didn't believe it neither. Still, I was no closer to knowing what did happen to Mama or why she left. Or if Mamaw Pickens was the kind of woman Miz Heckathorn thunk she was.

The sun beat down like hell-on-fire, and I reckoned it would'a dried up our old vegetable garden a heap. I needed to hurry and dig up the tomato plant.

But I wanted to go to Mamaw Pickens's grave first. If the gravestone proved that Miz Heckathorn was wrong about Mamaw traipsing off with some feller, it meant her memory wasn't so good no more. And if that was true, might be I did stay with 'em seven years back, and she jist forgot. I was plumb tired of being confused about ever'thing.

But the stone confused me even more:

JEFFERSON V. PICKENS, 1867–1923

LEONA M. (NÉE HAYWOOD) PICKENS, 1870–19

Nineteen what? No death year. I didn't know what to make of it. I leaned my shovel against a sturdy oak and run my fingers along Mamaw's name and her birth year, as though that would tell me something. The sun-warmed stone had no answers to give me.

Papaw had been dead for nine years. I couldn't recall a face to go with his name. I'da been jist four when he passed, but surely I had seen his face and held his hand. What had he looked like? Smelled like? Was his voice deep? My memories was as dead as he was.

But Mamaw—why was her dates unfinished? Was she still alive? Off somewhere "chasing squirrels"? And did Mama leave so she could chase squirrels, too? That didn't sound like the "good woman" folks said Mama was. Folks had to know more'n they let on.

A shadow come up behind me, and I thunk might be it was Norris until I heard the voice. "Nice day for a cemetery visit, isn't it?"

I spun around to face Mr. Grayson, the insurance peddler. He was a good head taller'n me, dang near blocking the sun. And he moved close to me, much too close.

"Visiting Mr. Pickens's grave, I see. What a nice thing for a granddaughter to do." His words was polite, but his face was cold as January and seemed to freeze me in place. My tongue couldn't find words. I tried to edge away from him, but my feet wouldn't move.

He set his hand on my shoulder. Shivers crept up my back and down my arms. "It's nice for a girl to show respect for her grandparents."

My mind was froze up, even in the hot sunshine. I had to do something, had to git out'a there, but I couldn't think clear.

"Does your father know you're here?" he asked.

That question scared the ice out'a my brain. "Of course he

does," I lied, and shrugged his hand off my shoulder. "Raynelle, too. And they's expecting me back directly."

"Your father should treat his children better than he does, don't you think?"

The feeling finally come back to my feet, and they edged slow, tiny steps. "Daddy's a good man," I said. Them words felt strange on my tongue, but I meant 'em.

Mr. Grayson didn't seem to notice I wasn't quite so close. He kept right on talking. "Did ya ever consider—"

A rustle in the grass distracted him, and he turned away from me. I took that chance to bolt and run, not looking back, fearing I'd hear the sound of him behind me, not slowing down until I reached the woods.

CHAPTER 27

THE TOMATO PLANT

In the shadow of trees, I stopped to catch my breath and looked back towards Mr. Grayson. I seen what that rustle in the grass had been. Norris Shortwell. Standing in front of Mr. Grayson with his lips flapping like always. I couldn't hear what Norris said, but I was never so glad to see him a-talking.

Good old Norris. He must'a follered me.

Mr. Grayson looked in my direction once, and I moved deeper into the woods. Peeking from behind the trunk of a broad maple, I seen that Norris seemed to make the man look right uncomfortable. *'Atta boy, Norris.*

When Mr. Grayson finally headed out'a the cemetery in t'other direction, I headed through the woods towards our old house. I looked behind me more'n once to make sure he hadn't follered. Finally reaching the hemlock grove, I heard a voice.

"Adabel, wait." It was Norris, and he was toting my shovel and bucket. "Ya forgot these."

I dang near reached out and hugged him. "Thank ya, Norris. Ya come along jist in time. That man gives me goose pimples."

"Me, too," he said. "I don't trust him. Though he always

seemed nice enough to Pick. Telling Pick he was smart enough to make a good living if he stayed out'a the mines."

"A good living doing what?" I asked.

"Selling insurance, I reckon."

I shrugged. "You know of folks that kin still afford insurance? I don't. Buying *food* is what folks think about."

"I s'pose some of 'em buy life insurance, on account of they ain't sure how long they kin survive. They want their families took care of if'n they don't. I do know Grayson always seems to have a pocketful of money."

I took the shovel and bucket. "Thank ya, Norris," I said again. "I got a plant to dig up."

"I'll come with you."

This time I didn't say no.

When I got home, Daddy follered me to the vegetable garden and watched me dig a hole for the new tomato plant. Afore he quit drinking, Daddy wouldn'ta noticed whether I come home without my head, but now he seemed to notice I was bothered up.

"It looks like a healthy tomato," he said. "Was things all right up at the old house when you was there?"

I lifted the plant from the bucket, careful to keep dirt around its roots. "Things was fine there," I said.

Daddy leaned down close as I lowered the new plant's roots into the hole. "If things was all right, how come you're jumpy as a meadow mouse?"

I wouldn'ta said nothing to a drunken Daddy, but the caring

look on his sober face loosed up my tongue. "I stopped by the cemetery and run into Mr. Grayson."

Daddy shot straight up. "Royce Grayson?" he bellowed.

I didn't know the man's first name. "I reckon. Is he the one what sells insurance?"

"He's the scoundrel that should be ashamed to show his face around Smoke Ridge. I don't want ya to never talk to him again. Ever!" Daddy yelled. "Ya hear me?"

Not talking to Mr. Grayson wasn't something I had to be told. "I hear, Daddy."

As I tamped dirt around the tomato plant, I remembered Pick telling me why Daddy give him that first shiner. Daddy forbid him to talk to somebody. And Pick refused to obey. Was that shiner on account'a Mr. Grayson?

Daddy watched me pour water around the plant. He took a deep breath, and when he spoke again his voice had lost its roar. "Ya does a good job with the garden, Adabel."

CHAPTER 28

MAKING DO

I fell asleep that night with Daddy's face in my head, the face that spoke them nice words about the work I done. I dreamed of Daddy saying other nice words, of him being kind and gentle. And I said nice words. *Daddy's a good man.* But Daddy's face turned mean and I seen him raise his fist.

I startled awake, sweat dripping down my face. The gentle Daddy had seemed so real. But I knew the Daddy that beat on Pick was truly real.

Daddy stayed sober and went fishing on his off-days, coming home with strings of redeyes and sun grannies. Raynelle fried the fish in lard, a delicious change from boiled cabbage.

Ever since the corn had disappeared, Raynelle'd been stretching company scrip like a rubber band fixing to snap, saving money by feeding us from our garden. Even if it meant eating the same thing ever' day.

When more green beans was ready, we had to save most of 'em for "shuck beans." I set on the porch three afternoons straight, stringing 'em for winter eating. I run the needle through the ends of dried bean pods like a necklace of beans. Necklace after necklace.

One meal's worth on each string. During the winter, Raynelle would soak a string of beans overnight to cook in lard for the next day's shuck beans. It almost made winter something to pine for.

Raynelle run her fingers along a string of beans and smiled. "When I git married, ya's goin' do jist fine," she said.

"Don't be gitting married no time soon. We need ya here." I would'a jumped up and clung onto her tight, but my lap was full'a beans.

❖

With Raynelle's clench on Daddy's hard-earned company scrip, we eked our way through summer and into fall. Cold weather snuck in for a day or two and we wrapped blankets around us and pulled up close to the cook stove until bedtime.

After school, Blissie gathered herbs and nuts. Back afore the Hard Times, we often fed beech and hickory nuts to our pig. It might'a been a good thing we didn't have a pig no more, on account'a that critter would'a starved plumb to death.

Me and Blissie spent hours cracking hickory nuts betwixt rocks, Blissie humming and smiling. We dug out the nut meats from the shells, plunking them into a bowl. Sometimes we plopped small pieces into our mouths.

"Ain't this a wonderful time of year?" Blissie said. I wished I could be as happy as she was, but I knew how hard food was to come by. And I still couldn't git through a meal without looking at Pick's empty chair and wondering if I'd ever see him again.

I had to be responsible like Raynelle, careful not to let a single scrap of shell git lost. We saved 'em in a basket for burning in the fireplace. They would make the fire last longer on cold winter nights. And give the fire's smoke a hickory smell.

My last year's shoes didn't fit me no more, and neither did Raynelle's old ones. She said we couldn't afford new ones. I had to squeeze my feet into them old shoes, even if my toes wasn't happy about it.

After a few painful days, warm weather come by for a visit. I shed my tight shoes and went barefoot again. But I knew the warmth wouldn't last, so I dug out a pair'a Pick's old shoes. I tried not to notice the pain of him being gone.

I showed Raynelle how they fit me. "Ya kin wear 'em at home," she said, "but ya cain't go to church in boys' shoes."

My toes could bear suffering in my old shoes one day a month. It'd give me something to think on besides Pastor Justice's sermon. The rest of the time, my feet walked in the same shoes Pick had, keeping him right underfoot and in my mind.

When the cold roared in like a coal train and stayed, Raynelle had to part with a goodly sum of company scrip for coal to keep us warm, and some evenings we had a fire in the fireplace. But the thing that warmed us most was having Daddy sober. He come through the worst of the D.T.'s and was like most other daddies. I wished I had a way to tell Pick.

CHAPTER 29

THE NICKEL

When November coated the windowpanes with frost, there was no more watering or weeding to do. Raynelle kept me busy with inside chores, but outdoors tugged at me.

One morning, Raynelle pulled me aside and tucked a nickel into my palm. A nickel! Smoke Ridge didn't make no five-cent scrip coins. This was real United States–minted money!

"Raynelle! Where'd ya git this?"

"Don't you worry none. Jist take it on up to the Baileys' place. They done a butchering yesterday, and ya kin buy some lard. Take a clean pail from the shed and tell 'em to fill it with a nickel's worth."

"Did ya git this nickel from Luddy Webster?"

"Where it come from ain't your business. How do you know I didn't git it from Daddy?"

"Daddy never give ya real money afore."

"That was the Daddy what needed drinking money." She put her hands on her hips. "Jist do what ya's told."

Sometimes I wondered if Mama'd been as bossy as Raynelle. I commenced the long walk towards the Baileys' with the nickel in my pocket, it and Raynelle on my mind. Was Daddy giving her actual money now? Or was Luddy? Or had it been hid away for a spell? Maybe since afore the Hard Times? Did Raynelle have more money hid away? Hid money wasn't likely. I almost wished Raynelle had stole the nickel somewheres. I'd rather her been a thief than beholden to Luddy Webster.

No answers on the nickel come to mind, so I quit chewing on the questions. Raynelle had entrusted me with real money, and it felt good traipsing through crackling leaves that crunched under my feet and rustled around me with ever' step. Each gust of wind showered more leaves down on my head.

The air was crisp, but not cold. I flung off the closed-in feeling of our shanty. Was this how Pick felt when he traipsed off? Had he been glad to git shed of our cramped house? And us? Would the pain of losing him ever ease its grip?

I tried to put troubling things clean out of my mind. But Mama dropped spang into my head. Questions never stayed away for long.

CHAPTER 30

MIZ BAILEY

By the time I come on the Baileys' place, the smell of ham crept through knotholes in the wood walls of their smokehouse. It was past noon, and my stomach spoke up loud as I watched little coils of smoke seep through ever' crack.

"Want to join us for our noon meal, Adabel?" Miz Bailey asked. "I's frying up sausage and sowbelly from yesterday's butchering." She didn't have to ask me twice.

Whilst we ate, Miz Bailey babbled on and on about other folks' business. She was a nice lady, but she seemed to thrive more on gossip than food. The Baileys was farmers, not miners, so the Mister didn't fetch home news from Smoke Ridge twice a week, and the Missus wanted to know ever'thing about ever'body.

When I scraped the last bite off my plate, Miz Bailey heaped it with more sowbelly, saying, "What has ya heard from your brother?"

"Pick don't write much," I answered and filled my mouth so full I couldn't talk. I didn't want us Cutlers to be fodder for chewing on at tomorrow's meal.

I repaid 'em for the food by staying to help wash dishes.

Miz Bailey's lips flapped the whole time I rinsed and dried the plates she handed me. Afore she could ask about Daddy, I changed the subject. "Did you know my Mamaw Pickens?"

"Most certainly. She broke a lot'a hearts in her young days, but Jeff Pickens seemed to settle her down. Ya know your daddy and her never seen eye to eye."

"On account of his drinking?"

"No, it weren't that. I don't think your daddy drank much afore your mama left. But Leona never thunk your daddy was good enough. She had other ideas about who her daughter should marry."

"Mamaw wanted Mama to marry somebody else?"

"The checkweighman down to the mine, as I recall."

I pictured the youngish man who weighed coal cars at Smoke Ridge Mine. "Mr. Fraley?"

Miz Bailey laughed. "Of course not. Joe Fraley was a boy at the time. The feller who was weighman back then was the same age as your daddy. And he sure did fancy your mama. But Ada never had eyes for no one but Ray Cutler."

"And ya remember my mama, do ya, Miz Bailey?"

She pulled a sudsy hand from her dishwater and wiped it on her apron. "I sure do."

"Do ya know what made her leave Smoke Ridge?"

"I knowed something was troubling her last I saw her, but she wouldn't talk about it."

I nearly dropped the wet cup I was fixing to dry. "Mama was troubled?"

"Seemed like."

"Miz Heckathorn said Daddy loved Mama deep."

She nodded. "They was head-over-heels for each other. But Leona never come around to Ada marrying Ray, so Ada stayed clear of her mama. Leastwise until Jeff got sick with the Black Lung."

"Papaw Pickens had Black Lung?" Why didn't I know that?

"Him and so many others. I'm right glad my man's a farmer."

"Miz Heckathorn said that soon as Papaw died, my mamaw lit out with somebody else."

"Plumb swept off her feet, as I recall. By him and his money. Money always makes a man look taller and handsomer." Miz Bailey chuckled at her own words.

Once more, my mind was spinning. I'd always thunk Mamaw was dead and buried beside Papaw. Why did it take so long to hear the truth? And why was my head so full of empty places?

CHAPTER 31

THE
STILL

I handed over Raynelle's nickel, and both the lard pail and me was brim-full as I headed towards home. And my head was brimming with questions. Questions about Mamaw and Papaw and a man with money who swept Mamaw off her feet. Questions about Mama and Daddy. If they was so head-over-heels in love, why did she up and leave?

Miz Bailey said Daddy didn't drink much afore Mama left. Was it the pain of losing her that drove him to drink? It seemed like love was a devil if it caused folks so much pain.

I didn't have time to paw through all them questions. The westward sun beamed down a warning. I had lollygagged too long in gitting to the Baileys' and listening to Miz Bailey talk, and now I'd be late gitting home.

Did I dare resort to the shortcut across Myrtle Henry's property? The old biddy didn't take kindly to trespassers. But I didn't want to make Raynelle cross neither.

Near-leafless trees didn't offer much cover, but I dared anyhow. Creeping through dry brush at the edge of Miz Henry's yard, I listened after each step I took, but the only noise come from me.

Her house looked quiet. No gnarled fingers pulled back a curtain or threw open the door. I hurried across the edge of the open yard and into the woods beyond it.

Once in the cover of trees, I breathed easier. But I walked quick-like, the need to git home pulling me along.

In the deepest part of the woods, I heard the *clank* of metal, and I smelt smoke. I peered around a big maple trunk. In a clearing no bigger'n a tablecloth, a fire brewed under a sizable contraption of containers, pans, and copper tubes. A man in overalls moved jugs and crocks under barrel spouts that set under the contraption.

I clamped my hand over my mouth to stifle the gasp that started to soar out of me. Copper coils twisted around and through that moonshine still, and my innards felt likewise twisted when I seen a shotgun leaning against a tree.

A row of empty Mason jars set on an upturned wood box, jist like the jars I seen behind the *For Sale or Rent* sign at our old house. Was this the moonshiner who used our old front porch as a drop place? There wasn't no jars behind the sign last time I was there. After Daddy quit drinking.

I held my breath and looked a tad closer at the man. Gray hair curled out from under his straw hat's brim and I watched the way his hand reached back to hitch up his drawers through the seat of his overalls. His behind had a familiar shape to it. A shape I had seen often. In the front pew at church. A shape wearing blue linen.

The moonshiner wasn't no man a'tall!

CHAPTER 32

THANKSGIVING

Miz Henry was making 'shine! Almost as unbelievable as Daddy not drinking it no more.

I snuck back through the woods quiet as moss on a rock, and steered clear of Myrtle Henry and her shotgun.

Raynelle didn't scold about me gitting home late. Her eyes was on the lard pail. "That's more'n a nickel's worth," she said. "Miz Bailey was mighty open-handed."

I didn't tell Raynelle that Miz Bailey was open-mouthed, too, and I didn't say nothing about what I seen up at Miz Henry's.

Now that Daddy was sober, Raynelle invited Mr. Webster and Lud to join us for Thanksgiving dinner. I hoped this invitation had nothing to do with a wedding announcement.

"Make sure Lud and his daddy git the good dishes," Raynelle told me as I set the table. The blue-flowered dishes was our only dishes, but I knew she meant to give 'em the ones with no chips or cracks. Since Pick and Daddy's fight broke two of our plates, we only had a couple "good" ones left.

Me and Blissie pulled Mama's trunk up to the table, so's Blissie'd have a place to set. I tugged a mite on the lid as we slid it across the floor. Locked. I'd tried to open that trunk time and again to see if any of Mama's paintings was inside, but it was always locked.

Blissie's usual chair would go to Mr. Webster. Lud set in Pick's chair, which bothered me considerable. I was still trying to git used to seeing it empty. But empty was a heap better'n Luddy Webster a-setting there.

Raynelle roasted a good-sized turkey, and its scent near-about drove me to grab a fork and knife and pull up a chair to the oven door. I put the carving knife and fork at Daddy's place and set down, jist itching to dig in. Raynelle carried the turkey, plump and golden-brown, to the table. Daddy looked at that turkey and up to Raynelle. She avoided his eyes as Mr. Webster pulled out her chair for her.

Daddy's gaze shifted to Mr. Webster. "Did ya have a sale on turkeys at the Grocery this week?"

"No," he said, "but I brung a pie for dessert."

Daddy looked at Lud, who jist stared back at him. "How much scrip did this here turkey cost us, Raynelle?" Daddy asked.

She looked down at her empty plate, whilst we all waited for the turkey to be carved. "It don't matter, Daddy," she mumbled. "Let's jist enjoy it."

"Raynelle?" His voice was as sharp as the carving knife.

Her voice come out mouse-quiet. "It didn't cost nothing, Daddy. The Quakers was giving away free turkeys to needy folks."

"Needy folks?" Daddy gripped the carving tools so tight, his veins stood out on his hands. "We's needy folks now?"

Raynelle's mouse turned into a bear. "We was *needing* a Thanksgiving dinner. And they was jist giving 'em away. Look how skinny your young'uns is since our corn got stole."

At the mention of the corn, Daddy's face clenched up and got red. I hadn't seen him lose his temper since he quit drinking, but the signs was all there.

"Ain't nothing wrong with accepting a little help now and again, Ray," Mr. Webster said in a calming voice.

Daddy was far from calmed. "My family don't take charity. I forbid any Cutler to eat a single bite of this ill-got bird."

"It ain't like I stole it, Daddy."

"What about that bowl of stuffing?" Daddy asked. "Quakers give ya that, too?"

"It's cornbread stuffing from the cornbread I baked last week. Don't ya recollect ya had two slices for Tuesday supper? I bought cornmeal from Mr. Webster." Raynelle looked at the grocer, and he nodded. "I had to buy it on account of *our* corn got stole."

Pick and Daddy had fought with their fists. Raynelle was fighting with words, making accusations with her tone.

Daddy ignored it. "What about them taters?" he asked.

"From our garden," Raynelle said.

"And the shuck beans?"

"The same."

We ate beans, stuffing, and potatoes for Thanksgiving dinner whilst that roasted turkey set on the table, wafting its smell up our noses.

"*I* got no problem with a little charity," Luddy said, reaching across me for the carving knife. Daddy's look could'a carved Lud into little pieces as Lud sliced him off a slab of turkey meat and ate it right in front of us. How could Raynelle even think about marrying a feller who done that?

We finished off our Thanksgiving dinner with the sweet potato pie Mr. Webster brung. It was a meal bigger'n we'd had in months, but it jist didn't seem filling enough with that turkey a-setting there mocking us.

"Do ya mind if'n Lonesome accepts a little charity, Daddy?" Raynelle asked. She didn't wait for an answer, jist cut off a chunk of meat for the dog. She walked with her head up, defiant, but she avoided Daddy's eyes as she toted the meat outside.

I reckon at least one Cutler enjoyed that Thanksgiving.

CHAPTER 33

SECRETS IN THE TRUNK

With Thanksgiving behind us, Raynelle's mind turned to thoughts of Christmas, even though it was still near a month off. Me and her was too grown to expect Christmas gifts, but we wanted something for Blissie.

Whilst Blissie was at school and Daddy at work, Raynelle crept into Daddy's room and come back with a key. She unlocked Mama's trunk, and we pawed through Mama's dresses.

"These ain't fitting dresses for Blissie," Raynelle said, running her fingers along the brown wool one. "But I kin cut this up to make a coat for Lula. And you could make the doll an apron from this lace collar. Your stitching ain't so bad no more."

I scrunched up my face.

"Or maybe you could make a hat," she said.

I didn't want to think about doll clothes. This was the first time Raynelle had opened Mama's trunk in months. I wanted to see if'n any of Mama's paintings was hid inside.

A roll of yellowed newspaper lay on the bottom of the trunk. I leaned in and reached for it. I could tell by the feel of it, something was inside.

The newspaper fell apart in my hands, revealing rolled-up canvas. "Look, Raynelle. A painting!" I unrolled it. "Two paintings!" Two pieces of Mama! Right here in our house!

I seen a big tree on one painting, but Raynelle took 'em from me afore I could look closer. She leaned against the trunk, and I set on the floor aside her. Together we looked at a painting of our old house. A man set in a chair on the porch, and a woman stood behind him with her hand on his shoulder. They was in old-fashioned clothes, and neither of 'em was smiling. Tight curls dangled from under the woman's hat.

"Is that Granny Cutler?" I asked.

Raynelle nodded. "Back in her young days." She pointed to the man. "And that's Granddaddy with her. Mama prob'ly painted that right afore they moved." Raynelle run her finger along the man's face. "When Granddaddy got the Black Lung."

"I thunk it was Papaw Pickens—Mama's daddy—who had Black Lung."

"Both of 'em did. Black Lung is the curse of being a miner. Granny and Mamaw was both widows from the Miner's Curse. Mama used to tell me not to marry a miner, even though *she* did. In Smoke Ridge, there ain't much choice. Mr. Clark, the blacksmith, is twice my age, and Mr. Fraley, the weighman, already has a wife and two young'uns. I reckon Mama'd be happy if I become a grocer's wife."

I didn't want to talk about Raynelle marrying up with Lud, and I felt a ripple of envy that she'd gotten advice from Mama.

"Do you think Mama was sorry she married a miner?" I asked. "Do ya reckon that's why she left?"

Raynelle thunk for a moment. "To be honest, I don't recollect

Mama ever being sorry she married Daddy. The two of them was like this." She held up two fingers squeezed together tight. "If a man loved me like Daddy loved Mama, I'd marry him in a minute, miner or not."

It was hard to think of Daddy as a man in love. "Miz Bailey said Mamaw Pickens didn't want Mama to marry Daddy," I said.

"I know Daddy was glad when Mamaw up and left. Them two was always crossways with each other."

"So you knew Mamaw ain't buried aside Papaw?" Why did she know things I didn't?

She nodded.

"But her name's on the gravestone."

"Sometimes they put both names on a stone at the same time. Makes it easier and cheaper when the next one dies."

"Even though she ain't dead yet?" It made me shudder to think about.

"Sometimes."

"It's peculiar having a body's name on a gravestone when they's still living. Do ya think she's *still* living?"

"She moved away years ago," Raynelle said. "Likely if she passed, she's buried where she moved to."

"How come you never told me none of this afore?"

She sighed and touched the faces of Daddy's parents. "I reckoned either ya remembered or ya didn't. Talking about 'em wouldn't bring 'em back. Why dig up old memories?"

At least she had memories.

CHAPTER 34

THE CLIMBING TREE

After one last look at Granny and Granddaddy on the porch of our old house, I rolled up that canvas to look at the tree painting under it.

The huge tree covered most of the canvas, and a girl with brown hair stood aside the trunk. Two other young'uns set on a bottom branch—two young'uns with red hair. Me and Pick! It had'a be us. And the brown-haired one was Raynelle. I run my fingers along the boy's face, jist like Raynelle'd done with Granny and Granddaddy on t'other painting. *Oh, Pick! Where'd ya go?*

"I couldn'ta been more'n eight when Mama painted that," Raynelle said. "That maple set at the edge of the woods near our old house. Pick called it the climbing tree, and he used'a climb it dang near ever' day. He'd go clean to the highest branches. And you al'ys tried to foller him. Mama made ya come down on account'a she was afeared ya'd fall and break your fool neck."

I squinted at them young'uns and tried to make the memory come into my head. I closed my eyes, and for a fleeting second, I seen a dizzying blur of leaves and branches. I felt like I was above 'em, looking down. Like Pick would'a been.

111

"I did climb that tree, Raynelle! I remember being way up high in it."

"That's right," she said. "Daddy told Mama that if'n ya was big enough to git on that bottom branch without help, ya was big enough to climb as high as your know-how let ya."

"I remember! I remember!"

The grin wouldn't leave my face, even though Raynelle looked at me like I was crazy. But she didn't know how hard it was a-living with those empty places in my head. I wanted to explain it to her, but right then, it was enough for me to have a memory to cling to.

Raynelle looked at the clock over the sink and the dresses heaped on the floor around us. "Blissie's goin' be home any minute. We need to git all this put back away."

I folded a green dress and added it to t'others, my smile spread clean across my face. I rolled up the tree painting and set it careful on the very top of Mama's dresses. Now that I knew the key was kept in Daddy's room, I knew I could git holt of it again and look at these paintings. Pictures with memories.

"If you was eight in that painting," I said, "I'da been jist four. To think I recollect climbing that tree when I was jist four."

"You was four in the painting," Raynelle said. "But you and Pick clumb that tree for years. I ain't sure how old ya was when ya first clumb all the way to the top. Might'a been eight or ten."

My smile shriveled and disappeared. Was I jist remembering something from a few years ago? From after Mama left? I wanted to believe it was more'n that.

CHAPTER 35

THE WHISTLE

I lay in bed at night thinking about that climbing tree, trying to picture my arms pulling me up into its branches. But I couldn't remember how old I'd been.

Another sound tread into our nights. Daddy. Coming home late. Whether it was Raynelle taking charity for Thanksgiving dinner or whether it would'a happened anyhow, Daddy started drinking again. Jist a little at first, so's all we noticed was the smell on his breath. But bad things happened on a cold, wet December day, and bad things had a way of leading Daddy down the moonshine path.

In a coal camp like Smoke Ridge, we was used to the sound of the mine whistle. On ever' working day, it signaled the beginning and end of a shift. A loud, unending, piercing shriek would'a meant an explosion or cave-in at the Smoke Ridge Mine.

But the whistle had an in-between sound, more'n a shift change, less'n a mine disaster. Three sharp blasts meant *help-is-needed, come-a-running.* Like if a young'un went missing, a house caught fire, or a neighboring town needed help. And since the blasts wasn't always easy to count, the way they echoed betwixt the hills, there'd be a pause and three more blasts.

That wet December Friday, I toted dishes to the table, fixing to set it for supper, whilst Raynelle boiled cabbage on the stove. Rain pattered on the shanty roof and drizzled down the windowpanes. I near-about dropped two plates when the first three blasts startled me. Me and Raynelle looked at each other and waited. Three more blasts.

"You go," Raynelle told me. "Blissie kin set the table. Take a jacket. The air's a-biting."

The first jacket my fingers latched onto used'a be Pick's. I threw it around my shoulders and raced out the back door, down the hill through the woods, slipping and sliding on wet leaves. Across the board over the creek, which was racing near as fast as I was. As I reached Smoke Ridge, I slowed my steps a mite and slid my arms into the jacket's sleeves.

Miz Sparks stood on the Dry Goods porch out of the rain and clear of the road's muddy puddles. "I ain't heard nothing yet," she called to me. "Make sure some'un comes back to let me know."

I nodded and kept going. I hurried past the school and on down Schoolhouse Hill, mud oozing down the hill with me. I run past Jane Louise's house, and on towards the mine.

The weighman's shack set jist outside the mine entry, where miners could push their full cars on the scale to be weighed. Rain pinged off the engine that powered the fans and pulleys, sending steam into the air like fog. The whistle stood atop a pole near the engine, and Mr. Fraley'd come from his weighman's shack and stood aside the whistle.

A sizable clump of men and boys and a few women gathered around, rain dripping off hat brims and noses.

Smoke Ridge miners emerged from the mine, even though

their shift hadn't ended. Daddy was amongst them. Wearing worried faces, they trudged through the mud to join the others near the whistle. I held my breath, waiting.

Words shot through the air like bullets, many gitting lost in the sound of rain, but a few found my ears.

"Explosion."

"Cave-in."

"Miners trapped."

"A mile-and-a-half deep."

I wedged through the crowd to Daddy's side. "Where?" I asked him.

"Zero Mine," he said. "In Yancey."

Was it on account of wearing Pick's jacket that the word *Yancey* seeped into my brain like it done? Teacher Bromley stayed in a room over at the Fields' place during the school year, but if'n her home in Yancey was empty, might be Pick was staying there and working in the mine for food money. Miz Bromley was the kind to let him do that.

I didn't say out loud what my brain was thinking, but I put my arm around Daddy's waist and hung on tight. He draped his arm around my shoulders and squeezed. I reached my other arm around him, touching my hands on Daddy's other side. Like a hug. The first shared betwixt us in longer'n I could remember.

Several men loaded tools on Mr. Putney's Ford truck to head down to Yancey and help with the rescue efforts.

Daddy said he was going with 'em. "Tell Raynelle I don't know when I'll be home."

"Be careful, Daddy." I reached for his hand. He gripped mine for a second and left.

Men filled the truck bed and hung onto the back. With a roar, it pulled away from the mine, tires spitting mud in their wake. Would miners be found alive? If Pick was in Yancey, could he be one of 'em, trapped in that mine with t'others? I jist stood there, rain drizzling down my face. One good thing about rain is tears don't show.

CHAPTER 36

ALL NIGHT

I bolted home and told Raynelle what Daddy'd said. "I'm going back to Smoke Ridge and wait for more news."

"Ya's a muddy mess. Ya cain't go out looking like that. And ya's soaked to the skin."

"No sense drying off when I'll jist git wet again." I tore out the door afore she could argue.

❖

Word come in slow over the course of the evening as I set on a bench near the weighman's shack, shivering in spite of Pick's jacket. A few women, young'uns, and old men set there, too. Ever'time a new message come in, one of the boys run up the hill to pass it along.

Rescuers had gone into the mine.

They found bodies.

Burnt bodies.

Bodies dead from black damp.

As a miner's daughter, I knew "black damp" was a deadly gas that hung in a mine after an explosion.

Dark settled in and night was on us, a black night with no

moon or stars, a black like the inside of a mine. Several of us still waited. Word finally come that bodies was being pulled out of Zero Mine. I leaned my head against the building and prayed like it was Sunday morning.

I prayed for Pick, but I must'a fell asleep on account'a I seen Daddy's face leaning over me, talking gentle words to me. Words like in Mama's swing poem. *Up in the air and down.* He wiped rain from my face with a cloth. I woke up, sucking on the sleeve of Pick's rain-soaked jacket, and Daddy was gone. It had been a dream, but it felt as real as the hard bench beneath me.

Daylight edged through rain clouds, and Miz Heckathorn found me asleep on the bench. I told her I was jist fine, but my chattering teeth told her otherwise. She took me to her house to dry off and give me some of Jane Louise's underwear and socks and one of her dresses to wear.

"Whilst ya git changed, I'll put breakfast on the table."

The smell of grits hung in the air of the one-room shack, and I saw flour, cornmeal, and soda on a shelf as I scrubbed mud off my legs at the sink. It made our shelves at home look plumb bare. I remembered the day I seen Miz Heckathorn peeling potatoes, whilst our potatoes at home come from Lud Webster and had bad spots.

Jane Louise didn't have a daddy no more. Did she git food from Chester Putney like Raynelle did from Lud? Or did the Heckathorns take charity from the Quakers?

"It's jist horrible about the disaster down to Yancey, ain't it?" Miz Heckathorn said.

I didn't trust my mouth to speak about it, but I nodded.

Jane Louise put plates on the table and acted like nothing had changed betwixt us, like we was still friends and seen each other jist yesterday.

I slipped the borrowed dress over my head, and its hem dropped well past my knees. Jane Louise giggled and pointed at me. "My dress is too big for ya, Adabel. Ya's skinny as a starved dog."

"That ain't nice, Jane Louise," her mama scolded.

"It's all right, ma'am," I said. "I al'ys been skinny." *And us Cutlers don't take charity.* "Thank ya for the dress."

I was polite to her mama, but it didn't set right for Jane Louise to feel sorry for *me.* I looked around the room, at anything other than Jane Louise's pitying face.

A bed in the corner was covered with a worn spread, and a shelf hanging above the bed held a framed photograph of Jane Louise's daddy and a book bound in blue. The book reminded me of one Daddy kept aside the family Bible in his room at home.

"Set yourself down, Adabel," Miz Heckathorn said. "Breakfast is near-about ready."

I pounced on them grits jist like that starved dog Jane Louise had spoke of. Her mama even dished seconds. I hadn't had seconds of anything since the day-after-butchering meal up to the Baileys'.

"Ya heard from your brother?" Jane Louise asked. It was the same question Miz Bailey had asked.

I answered Jane Louise with a head shake. After the Zero Mine disaster, I wasn't sure Pick was even still alive. *Stop stuffing yourself with grits, Adabel,* I told myself. *Ya need to find your brother.* I swallowed. *For better or worse, find him!*

Shoving the last spoonful into my mouth, I got up from the table with a garbled "Thank ya, ma'am."

"Ya ought to stay and rest a spell," Miz Heckathorn said.

"I would, ma'am, but like as not, Raynelle's worried sick by now. I best git on home."

I headed up Schoolhouse Hill whilst she stood at her front door and watched me go. Soon's I reached the school at the top, where she couldn't see me no more, I turned away from the path that would'a took me to our shanty.

I edged along the side windows of the school and down through the woods behind it. Clinging to wet vines and bushes, I slid down the muddy path to the railroad tracks. I stepped from one tie to the next and come up to the mine from t'other direction. Back to that bench by Mr. Fraley's shack. Mr. Fraley wasn't there. Likely, he went down to Yancey with t'others.

I set there all morning, knowing Raynelle would wonder where I was. But I had to see if word come about Pick.

Corky Danfield sauntered over. "Ain't no sense in staying here," he said. "No more news. All the bodies has been recovered. Twenty-three of 'em."

Fear pierced my gut as I let out a low whistle through my teeth. "They all been identified?"

"Ain't heard."

"Then I guess there might could be more news."

He shrugged like I was jist plain stupid, and turned to go.

"Hey, Corky. Ya know where they's taking them bodies?"

He turned back around. "My daddy said they's taking 'em to the mortuary down in Harlan."

"Kin ya tell me how to git there? I need to go."

CHAPTER 37

BODIES IN HARLAN

Corky give me an annoyed look. "Why in tarnation ya want to go where the bodies is?"

"Cain't ya jist answer my question?"

"My daddy might let me take ya in his Model A if'n ya really hanker to go there. Want I should ask 'im?"

"If ya would, Corky, I'd be grateful."

A grin stretched across his face. "Grateful enough to give me a kiss?"

I blew out my breath. "Men has *died*, Corky, and that's what ya think about?"

"*I* think about kissing, and *you* think about gitting to Harlan. What'da ya say? We got a deal?"

"Only a kiss on the cheek," I said.

"On the lips or it don't count."

I blew out my breath again.

"That's my price," he said.

"Tell me the way to Harlan and I'll git to walking."

"All right, you mule-headed girl. How's about ya kiss me on the cheek, but I tell Jane Louise ya kissed me on the lips? And you cain't tell her otherwise."

And Corky thunk girls was deceitful. "No kiss until ya ask your daddy about the Ford."

He drove up ten minutes later in his Daddy's 1928 Model A.

"Git in," he said, "and pay the price."

I clumb up into the Ford and plunked down aside Corky. I'd only ever been in an automobile one time, when me and Pick went with Teacher Bromley to fetch some books from her home in Yancey, but I didn't say so. The car trembled a mite, kind of like a coin does right afore it stops spinning.

Corky leaned towards me, and I lightly brushed his cheek with my lips.

"Ya call that a kiss?" he said.

"I never claimed to be no expert."

It was Corky's turn to blow out *his* breath afore he ground the gears and the Ford rumbled down the road, away from Smoke Ridge Mine. I warmed my cold, wet feet against the fireboard that separated the inside of the auto from the engine. We drove across the railroad tracks, and my teeth dang near rattled loose. The roads was slick, and Corky had to watch his driving careful-like. We was both quiet for a long time.

"Good thing the rain stopped," Corky said after a spell. "I ain't drove much in rain."

We crossed a concrete bridge on Main Street in the town of Harlan, and crowds of folks left no question about where the bodies was. But automobiles lined both sides of ever' street. Finding a place to park wasn't easy.

We drove past the Citizens National Bank three times, that

bank Daddy told us about in January. A grand building, closed near a year now, reminding folks it was Hard Times. Boarded-up stores offered more reminders. A furniture store. A jewelry store. A couple restaurants.

Corky brought the Ford to a stop more'n four blocks from where crowds gathered. We walked the rest of the way, passing houses and stores, more of 'em empty than not. A naked mannequin lay on its side in the window of a dark clothing store, a mannequin with no head. Shivers gripped me as I hurried by and tried not to think about dead bodies—even though I was about to look at some. I couldn't make myself erase the thought from my mind. Men had died and I was fixing to look at bodies to see if Pick was one of 'em.

Cumberland Hardware and Undertaking Establishment was where the bodies was. On the second floor over the hardware store. The stairs was thronged with men, women, and young'uns. White folks and colored folks both. Plenty wore their Sunday best, but others was dressed no better'n me—in Jane Louise's too-big dress and Pick's jacket and old shoes.

I got in line to start up the steps and seen tears in the eyes of many. I even heard wailing from the second floor.

"Ain't it sad?" said a lady on the step above me. "Twenty-three lives all snuffed out at once."

"So sad," I agreed. "Do ya know was they all identified?"

The lady nodded. "Six was brothers."

Corky stood behind me on the steps, his eyes big.

I finally reached the second floor, where new widows wept openly and held onto small young'uns. Older women, who must'a lost sons, cried on the shoulders of their husbands, who dabbed at their eyes and noses with handkerchiefs.

I tried to look around other folks to see the bodies. Did any

123

of 'em have red hair? Corky grabbed my hand, and I didn't make him let go.

Following the line that snaked between the rows of bodies, I saw faces of the dead. Up close. Most looked like they was jist asleep and might wake up any minute. About half was colored.

The bad-burnt bodies had their faces covered. I didn't realize I was squeezing Corky's hand until he squeezed back.

Each body had a name on a card. And none of the names was Pickens Haywood Cutler.

CHAPTER 38

MUD

Me and Corky walked back to the Model A.

"Imagine six brothers dying at one time," he said.

"A tragedy," I said, the sight of them dead miners still stuck in my brain, and the faces of them widows with young'uns scraping me raw inside. I comforted myself with the reminder that none of them was *my* brother.

Corky clumb up into the Ford afore me and slid across the seat. By the time I was in and closed the door, the Model A rumbled to life.

We rode in silence a spell, afore Corky said, "I reckon life'll be hard on them women with young'uns, losing a husband like that."

I pulled Pick's jacket tight around me and said in a quiet voice, "It's hard for anybody to lose a spouse. When a man loses his wife, too."

"But there wasn't no . . . oh, you mean your daddy losing your mama. But she didn't die in a mine explosion or nothing. She jist lit out."

My temper flared. "She's gone all the same. And nobody kin tell me why."

125

"There's rumors," he said.

"What rumors? I ain't heard no rumors."

"My mama said *your* mama was fixing to have a baby at the time."

"That's jist plumb stupid." I crossed my arms over my chest. "If a woman was goin' have a baby, that'd be the wrongest time to up and leave."

Corky looked sidewise at me. "Not if it wasn't your daddy's baby."

"She wasn't like that!" I didn't truly know *what* my mama was like, but I couldn't jist set there and listen to him talk about her that way. Even if he *was* driving. I punched his shoulder. Hard. The Ford lurched and almost drove off the road.

"Dang, Adabel!" He cut the wheel back towards the center of the road. But the car wouldn't move. He ground gears and tried again, but the Ford was stuck in mud at the edge of the road.

Corky swore some of the awfulest words I ever heard, and they was aimed at me. The not-swearing part was, "Ya fool girl. Ya asked about rumors and I jist answered ya. It ain't my fault what folks said."

He told me to git behind the wheel whilst he pushed the Ford out'a the mud.

"I don't know how to drive," I said.

"Well, ya either got to drive or push."

He set the parking brake, and I slid over behind the wheel.

"This here's the clutch." He pointed. "Hold it in whilst ya give it the gas. Don't let off'n the brake until I tell ya. And don't let it roll back'ards or ya'll run over me."

I admit it was a tempting thought.

"I don't know about this, Corky." The gas pedal was small and round. And near out'a reach of my foot.

"Jist try. I'll tell ya when."

He disappeared behind the car, and I readied my foot on the clutch.

He yelled, "Now!"

I pressed the button on the parking brake, and moved the gear shift like Corky done showed me. I stretched out my leg to push on the gas. The engine made almost as much noise as Corky, who swore like the devil.

"Try again! Now!"

This time the Ford jerked forward a little.

"Give it a little more gas!"

I pushed harder on the small, round pedal, and the Ford pulled out'a the mud and bolted up the road.

"Shove in the clutch and stomp on the brake!"

I confess I thunk about keeping on like I hadn't heard him. Jist drive on up that road, leaving Corky Danfield in the mud watching me disappear around the bend.

CHAPTER 39

NORRIS FETCHES ME HOME

I noticed Corky wore a heap of mud when he clumb back in the Ford. He didn't say a word, but the look on his face swore.

The sun had dropped behind the hills by the time we drove up to Smoke Ridge Mine. The polite thing would'a been to thank Corky for taking me to Harlan, but he made me so dang mad. And I'd already *paid* him for the ride.

I threw open the door and jumped out as soon as the car stopped. It was goin' be dark by the time I walked clean home, but I didn't want Corky to take me no farther. I was fixing to let loose a string of my own swear-words, when I heard my name.

"Adabel Cutler. Folks are worried about you. I can give you a ride. My Buick is right here."

I'da been happy for a ride with most anybody that wasn't Corky, but it was the tall shadow of Mr. Grayson that stood out against the not-quite-dark sky.

I edged back from the man, but could only go as far as the door of the Model A, and Corky was fixing to drive away.

I was fumbling for the door handle so I could climb back inside, when headlights of a truck barreled towards us. They come to a halt, and a familiar figure jumped down from the driver's seat.

"Adabel! Where you been? I come to fetch ya home. I got Mr. Putney's truck." Norris Shortwell. The boy who always seemed to come to my rescue.

"I can drive her," Mr. Grayson said.

I latched onto Norris's arm. "I'll go with Norris."

We hurried to the truck, and I clumb up onto the seat, shivering with something more than the night air's chill.

The shadow of Mr. Grayson ambled away into the dark, and I let out a breath of relief.

Norris got behind the steering wheel and looked over to me. "Your daddy's dang near busted a gasket with worry."

"With worry or with drink?" I asked.

"He ain't had a drop that I kin tell. Raynelle's worried, too. I told 'em I'd fetch ya home."

For a girl who hadn't been in an automobile more'n once afore today, I sure was making up for it. Norris drove better'n Corky, keeping the truck right smack in the middle of the muddy road. He didn't ask where I'd been, but for some reason, I felt I owed him an answer to the question he didn't ask.

"Corky took me down to Harlan to see the dead miners."

He didn't say a word. Jist eased the truck around one hill, changed gears, and headed up another.

"I jist had to see 'em," I said. "I was scared one of 'em might be Pick."

He looked at me in the dark truck for a second and turned his eyes back to the road. "Why didn't ya ask me? I could'a told ya Pick wasn't one of 'em."

"What? You know where Pick is?" If anybody knew where Pick was, it'd be Norris.

"I didn't say that," he said. "But you know as well as me that

129

Pick wouldn't work in a mine."

"He wouldn't *want* to work in one. And he'd never work for Smoke Ridge, side by side with Daddy, but if he's on his own, he has to earn money somehow."

"Pick's right smart. He'd manage." He paused afore he added, "You know Pick cares about his kin, right?"

"He don't act like it."

He give me a sidewise glance just afore the truck's headlights picked up rows of miners' shanties. None of the miners I knew owned automobiles, so headlights was cause for curtains to be pulled back and faces to appear behind window glass.

Stopping in front of our shanty, Norris said, "I hope ya got a better excuse for your daddy than ya went down to Harlan to look at dead bodies."

He come around and opened the truck door, as the shanty door flew open.

"Where the devil ya been?" Daddy roared, and pulled me close at the same time. He gripped me so hard I thunk my bones would break, but I breathed in the smell of coal dust and hugged my daddy for the second time in two days.

"I'm right sorry, Daddy," I mumbled into his shirt, feeling his arms tight around me. "I didn't mean to be gone so long."

To my shock, Daddy didn't demand an answer to his question. "Git yourself to bed," was all's he said when he finally let me go. He went over to thank Norris and I went inside.

Daddy didn't come home until late that night, and he was so drunk he didn't make it to bed. He passed out on the floor with his face planted in the rag rug in front of Mama's trunk.

CHAPTER 40

CHURCH

I'd gone to bed like Daddy'd said, but I'd shivered and shuddered with cold for a long time, lying betwixt my sisters. By the time I heard Daddy come in, I was feeling cozy from Blissie and Raynelle's warmth, but something made me git up and see to him. I slid out from the end of the bed and pattered my bare feet across the chilly plank floor.

Leaning Daddy up against the trunk, I wiped his face with a wet rag and dried it with a towel. I helped him to his room and onto his bed. Afore going back to my own warm bed, I pulled a cover over him.

In the past, we always let Daddy sleep off his drink and tend to his own morning-afters. But this binge was my fault. If I hadn't traipsed off with Corky, afeared my brother had been kilt in a mine explosion, Daddy wouldn'ta had no reason to drink.

"Only one to blame for Daddy's drinking is Daddy," Raynelle said whilst we ate breakfast. "Nobody made him head back down that moonshine path. And don't never tell him ya went looking for Pick."

I'd told her afore I went to bed where I'd gone and why. *She* hadn't let Daddy's question go unanswered. She'd scolded me in that mama-like way of hers, afore she hugged me tight. Jist like Daddy done.

"Why would he mind me looking for Pick?"

"It would jist remind him what his drinking's done to this family. And that'd likely drive him right back into the bottle. Now git yourself ready for church."

Church! I'd plumb forgot it was Sunday. Of all Sundays, why did it have to be a Church Sunday? Though I reckoned I ought'a thank God for a few things.

I poked up the fire and let the iron warm whilst I dug out my cleanest dress. Raynelle brushed Blissie's hair, and I squeezed my toes into my too-tight shoes.

We walked into Smoke Ridge, where the school's bigger classroom had been made ready for church. Pews, usually stored in the basement, was lined up in neat rows, and desktops had been lowered to make extra seats in back.

It was the first Church Sunday since I took the shortcut across Miz Henry's property last month. I watched her blue linen dress and my mind pictured overalls across her ample backside. I had to clamp my mouth shut to keep from laughing.

I wished Pick was beside me in the pew, so's I could elbow him and point. It was the kind'a thing the two of us would'a shared and laughed about.

After two verses of "Bringing in the Sheaves," Pastor Justice led a prayer for the families of the dead miners in Yancey.

"Widows will need the Lord's help to git through these Hard Times without husbands to look after 'em," he said. "And parents are writing *December ninth, 1932* in their family Bibles to mark the death date of sons."

I bowed my head and recollected all them widows, young'uns, and parents I seen in Harlan. Families with empty places.

When the sermon was fixing to start, I added another little prayer that it wouldn't be on drinking or honoring thy father. No matter what Raynelle said, I was feeling blameful enough for one day.

But the sermon kept on with the subject of death and not knowing when God might call us Home. I wondered if Mama'd already been called. If she was dead, that would explain why she never come back from wherever she run off to. It was almost a comforting thought that Mama might be dead. It was better'n feeling she didn't love us enough to come home.

After the service, folks shook hands with the pastor on the steps and exchanged howdies with one another on the wet grass. We shook Pastor's hand, and he knew not to ask where Daddy was. Folks never had trouble talking *about* us Cutlers, but nobody said much of anything *to* us. Except Lud Webster, who took holt of Raynelle's hand right out in front of God, Pastor Justice, and the whole congregation.

It sickened me the way he leaned in close to her, put one hand on the small of her back. I wanted her to pull away, but she didn't. I turned my head so's I didn't have to watch 'em, and the corner of my eye caught Miz Heckathorn talking all friendly-like with Myrtle Henry.

I walked up to Jane Louise. "Come wash day, I'll clean your dress and things, so's I kin give 'em back to ya fresh."

"I ain't in no hurry," she said. "It was a' old dress."

"Thank ya for lending 'em to me all the same." My voice didn't sound like mine, talking like a polite stranger with somebody who used'a be my friend.

"You ain't heard from Pick?" she asked.

Her asking about Pick reminded me *why* we'd been friends. She jist used me to friendly up to my brother. Manners fled. "Ya want I should tell Chester Putney ya asked after my brother?"

"Chester went back home on Thursday. He'd already stayed longer'n he was s'posed to." The sadness in her words almost made me feel bad for her. Almost.

"Oh," I said. "If Pick was back, ya'd be my friend again?"

"Adabel Cutler! What a mean thing to say!"

Our voices had gotten loud. Folks turned to stare at us. But I didn't care. I recollected how Jane Louise didn't come around no more after Pick left, how she'd felt sorry for me when she lent me her dress.

My temper jumped up into my throat and come out in my words. "By the way, Jane Louise, if Corky tells ya I kissed him, the truth is he kissed me first and said it was a heap better'n kissing you."

I turned away from her open-mouth gasp and walked out of Smoke Ridge as fast as my painful shoes would let me.

CHAPTER 41

RAYNELLE'S NEWS

Daddy was still sleeping it off when I slipped into the shanty and sloughed off my painful shoes. I set barefoot on the cold back porch whilst I scraped mud off Pick's old shoes that I'd wore to the mine and down to Harlan.

"Dang it, Pick!" I said to his shoes. "Where are ya? I need ya here." I slid the shoes on my feet, hoping to feel a closeness to my brother, but they was jist old shoes. The feel of Pick was gone from 'em.

I stoked the stove from the coal scuttle to warm the room, and recollected Pastor's words about family Bibles. Was births and deaths listed in ours? If Mamaw Pickens was dead, would her death date be wrote inside it? If Mama couldn't read, ain't likely she could write. But Daddy knew how, and he kept the family Bible in his room—where he was sleeping off his drink.

I put my ear to his door and listened. He was snoring. Could I slip in there and peek in the Bible afore Raynelle and Blissie got home? I was still trying to gather some gumption, when the back door flew open, and Blissie stood there. Alone.

I moved away from Daddy's door. "Where's Raynelle?" I whispered.

"With Lud. Said for you to git Sunday dinner started."

"And did she say what I was s'posed to cook?"

She shook her head.

At breakfast, we'd finished off the meager bread, baked more'n a week ago. And I didn't see no beans soaking. Rummaging through the nearly bare cupboard, I dug into the potato sack and pulled out four of 'em. I cut 'em up with their skins still on and put 'em on to boil. Raynelle expected me to do her work whilst Lud dang near pawed all over her in front of church. *I* boiled long afore the taters did.

The fire was hot and the potatoes near to boiling when Raynelle hurried in, her nose and cheeks red from the cold.

"I hope potatoes is all right for dinner. Ya didn't tell Blissie what I was s'posed to cook."

She nodded, but didn't say nothing. She kept rubbing her hands together.

My temper cooled in the chilly air that follered her inside. "Come warm your hands at the stove," I told her, but she didn't seem to hear. I grabbed holt of her arm and tugged her over to the stove. "Why don't ya finish these taters? That'll warm ya up."

She didn't reach out. Jist kept rubbing her hands together like she was washing 'em, but with no sink and no water.

When I looked closer at her hands, I seen the ring. A gold ring with a yellow stone.

Something fearful clutched at my innards. "Raynelle, where'd ya git that ring?"

"Lud give it to me. Asked me to marry him." Her words come out plain. Not a hint'a joy in 'em.

"Well, I hope to Glory ya said no." The fearful something inside me twisted and turned.

136

Her voice got all high-pitched and squeaky. "If I said no, would I be wearing his dead mama's ring?"

"Ya don't look happy about it."

Afore she could say anything, Daddy stepped from his room, one overall strap up and one down, barefoot. He was the color of boiled cabbage, gray with a tinge of green.

"Raynelle's goin' marry Lud Webster," Blissie told him.

Daddy lurched over to the sink, retching and gagging and throwing up whatever was in him, stinking up the room to Kingdom Come. But I had to admit, Raynelle's news made me feel like doing the same dang thing.

CHAPTER 42

SUNDAY DISHES

Daddy cleaned up his own mess. I watched him from the stove as he done it. A disgusted look turned to one of sadness and hung heavy on his face. Was it on account'a Raynelle's news? Was he as worried as me about another empty place in our house? His eyes was red, but something else in those eyes reached out and pulled me in.

I recollected the dream I'd had that night on the bench by the weighman's shack. I'd dreamed of a sad, gentle Daddy who wiped rain from my face. It'd seemed like more'n a dream. And that Daddy had seemed more real than the Daddy who wiped up vomit and cleaned hisself up for Sunday dinner.

It was a quiet meal. Raynelle didn't talk about Lud's proposal, didn't look like no happy bride-to-be. If a boy ever talked marriage with Jane Louise, she'd jabber and gush and flaunt her ring. Raynelle jist spooned boiled taters into her mouth in silence.

When Daddy and Blissie went outside to fetch firewood, me and Raynelle washed dishes. She slid off the yellow-stone ring and set it on the shelf above the sink.

"Why ya got to marry Luddy?" I asked straight out.

She scrubbed at a plate that looked right clean already. "On account'a he asked."

"Ya could'a said no."

"And then what? He'd stop coming around, stop bringing food from the Grocery. We need ever' scrap he gives us."

Gitting "scraps" from Luddy Webster seemed a whole heap worse'n taking a handout from the Quakers. I wondered if Daddy knew Raynelle took charity from the grocer's son.

"If I marry Lud, I kin move in with him and his daddy," Raynelle went on. "I'll cook for the two of 'em, and put food aside for you. And ever' bite will last longer without me here."

"Pick said that, too. That the food would stretch further with him gone. But I'd give up eating forever and ever to have him home again."

"That's crazy talk." Raynelle looked up from a sudsy plate. "I got to do this."

I took the plate from her afore she had a chance to wash the blue flowers clean off it. "Do ya truly love Lud, Raynelle?"

"He's good to me."

"That ain't what I asked."

"Ya's too young to understand, Adabel."

"Then I'm too young to take care of this here house and family without ya."

"Don't fret over it. I'll teach ya what ya need to know afore me and Lud gits married. The way Granny Cutler taught me."

I lugged the dishpan outside to dump its dirty water over the porch rail, Raynelle's words chewing at my gut. I couldn't let her marry Lud. She didn't even love him. I'd have to be right slow at learning to take over. Might be if I dragged my feet enough, Lud would git tired of waiting.

CHAPTER 43

BAD BLOOD

I hung the dishpan on its wall peg and carried the rinse pan outside to empty it. Blissie and Daddy come up from the woods, and Blissie toted her armful of wood inside. Daddy dropped his on the ground by the woodpile and called me over.

He used his angry voice, even though he hadn't had a drink since last night. "Didn't I tell ya never to talk to Royce Grayson?"

My voice come out quiet. "Yes, Daddy."

"The Shortwell boy said ya was talking to Grayson when he found ya last night."

My voice gathered some steam. "I didn't talk to the man, Daddy. Honest. He talked to me, but I didn't say nothing back."

"What did he say to ya?"

"He offered me a ride home. He was jist standing there when me and Corky pulled up. But I wasn't goin' go with him. I swear I wasn't." I was afeared Daddy would ask where I'd been with Corky, but his mind was stuck on Grayson.

"He was already there?" Daddy looked away for a minute, and I could see he was thinking. "The day ya run into him at the cemetery, was you there first? Or him?"

I thunk back. "I didn't see him when I got there, but when I was at Papaw Pickens's grave, there he was—behind me. Scared me the way he come up quiet like that."

Daddy shook his head fierce and doubled his fists, but I knew he wasn't riled with *me*. "He must'a follered ya there."

"But why, Daddy? Why would he do that?" I knew he didn't foller me from Harlan, but if he'd been lurking and seen me leave with Corky, he had'a know we'd come back sooner or later. Thinking that a growed man slunk around, watching and follering, give me shivers that sent ice clear to my bones.

Daddy clenched and unclenched his hands. "I don't trust that man any further'n I could fling a mule in full harness. You jist keep away from him."

I nodded so hard my teeth rattled. "Yes, Daddy."

He put his hand on my shoulder, and I felt its warmth right through my dress. "You ain't at fault, Adabel. There's been bad blood betwixt me and Royce Grayson for near-about twenty years. But I didn't think he'd carry his grudge to my family."

"Twenty years?"

"Near-about. He was checkweighman back then, and shorted me on my tonnage time and again. When I could prove it, I reported him to Putney and got him fired. A miner's got to be able to trust the man who weighs the cars."

Daddy give my shoulder a pat afore he moved away and turned to the woodpile. "You run along inside, Adabel, and don't worry none. I think me and Royce needs to talk."

Don't worry none? I hoped Daddy wouldn't git all liquored up afore he talked to Grayson. I wondered if Norris telling him about Grayson was what brung on Daddy's binge last night.

I didn't recollect Mr. Grayson being weighman, but it wasn't like I forgot. Twenty years ago I wasn't even born yet. It was hard to picture someone else doing Mr. Fraley's job. Fraley was the only checkweighman I knew.

As I carried the empty pan inside, I remembered talk of another weighman. Reaching to hang the pan on the wall, the jumbled thoughts of two weighmen fell clearly into place. The pan slipped from my fingers and clanged to the floor. I gathered it up quick and ignored Raynelle's scolding look.

Daddy'd said Mr. Grayson was the checkweighman twenty years ago. And Miz Bailey'd said Mamaw Pickens wanted Mama to *marry* a checkweighman!

CHAPTER 44

TROUBLESOME THOUGHTS

I had trouble sleeping that night. My thoughts jumbled together. Was Mr. Grayson the man Mamaw'd wanted Mama to marry? Would Daddy pick a fight with Mr. Grayson? If the two of 'em got in a fight—a real bad, drunken fight—Daddy could end up hurt or in jail.

But Miz Heckathorn's words about "chasing squirrels" kept coming back to me. Did Mama pick up and run off with Mr. Grayson? That didn't sound like the Mama folks talked of, the good woman who loved Daddy even though he was a miner. And if Mama'd run off with Mr. Grayson, why would he still come to Smoke Ridge a-nosing around? And why was he follering *me*?

My lack of sleep left me tired the next day, but tired don't stop Raynelle when she sets her mind to something. She started my lessons on taking over the household chores anyhow. Blissie was at school, and Raynelle measured Lula afore she cut into Mama's old brown dress. "With a doll, I can cut exact," she said. "If ya's making a dress for Blissie, cut it big, leave some extra fabric in the seams and hem for letting out as she grows."

I tried to hold back a yawn, and Raynelle lit into me.

"Ya got to learn this," she said. "This household is goin' depend on you."

My mind was far away from sewing lessons, and I wasn't goin' let it take on the subject of Raynelle leaving. I run my fingers along the roughness of the brown dress. "Mama might'a left her dresses behind on account'a they wouldn't fit no more if'n she was expecting a baby."

Raynelle's mouth fell open. "What makes ya think Mama was goin' have another baby?"

"Corky Danfield said so."

"How would he know?"

"Heard his folks a-talking."

She stared at the dress in her hands, but I could tell she wasn't seeing it. Her mind was remembering back to a time that my mind didn't have recollection of. I set quiet and let her think.

"Mama was feeling peaked afore she left," she finally said. "She *had* gotten a tad round. Might be she *was* goin' have a baby."

"Miz Bailey said Mama seemed troubled about something last time she seen her. You know what that something might'a been? Would having a baby been cause for worry?" I didn't mention what Corky'd accused Mama of.

Raynelle let out a sigh. "Could'a been. Mama had a rough time giving birth ta Blissie. And did ya know there was another baby? Younger'n you, but afore Blissie. A little boy. Born dead, he was. They named him Jefferson for Papaw Pickens."

I'd had another brother I didn't even know about! How could I not know? I felt the pain of one more empty place digging a hole inside me. I wiped a tear from my cheek. Raynelle was planning to leave another empty place. *No! No more empty places.*

"What would Mama say about you marrying Lud?" I asked.

Raynelle twisted that yellow stone around and around on her finger. "I think she'd say I was doing what has to be done. Mama didn't want me to marry a miner. And she always believed in doing what was best for the family."

"And she thunk it was best to up and leave us?"

"I know it don't seem so, but somehow she must'a felt it was."

She stared up at the ceiling as if Mama was up there. "My last memory of Mama was her leaning over my bed. I was jist about to fall asleep and she kissed my forehead and said . . ." A tear run down her cheek, too.

"Said what?"

Raynelle wiped her eyes. "At the time, I thunk she said 'Good night,' but I realized later it was 'Good-bye.'"

CHAPTER 45

SPINNING

Raynelle turned ever' household chore into a lesson. When she cooked, she showed me how to keep the fire low under a pan of lard. "Ya don't want it to git too hot and burn," she said.

I didn't want to think about lard and cooking. The things that troubled my mind kept me awake at night. "You and Luddy ain't goin' git married anytime soon, are ya?"

"Not until after Christmas."

I gasped. "Raynelle, Christmas is less'n two weeks away. Ya cain't git married until after *next* Christmas. Or maybe the one after that."

She jist shook her head at me.

I couldn't imagine our shanty without Raynelle. Even though she got bossy with us, she was closest to a mama me and Blissie had.

Raynelle sent me to the Grocery to fetch some flour and baking soda. She was thinking ahead to baking something special for Christmas dinner. I didn't want to think about Christmas—or what would come after. And I didn't want to go someplace I might run into Mr. Grayson.

"Wouldn't *you* druther go?" My tone was a mite sassy. "So's ya kin see your future husband?"

Instead of scolding me for my sass, she jist said, "I reckon we'll see plenty of each other once we's married."

I chafed at the way Raynelle didn't behave like a body fixing to git married and spend her whole entire life with someone. If she'da seemed happy about it, might be I could'a scraped up a bit of sisterly gladness for her.

❖

I walked fast down to Smoke Ridge, my eyes on the path in front of me and my ears alert for the sound of footsteps a-follering me. But there was no sign of Mr. Grayson, and I let myself breathe easier when I walked into the Grocery.

Lud was behind the counter. "If it ain't my future sister-in-law," he said.

I felt a shiver from his words, but tried not to show my feelings. "I seen the ring ya give Raynelle. She said it was your mama's."

"It was. My daddy give it to her afore they got married."

"The ring must'a meant a lot to ya. And to your daddy." I s'pose Lud truly cared about Raynelle.

"She wore it till the day she died," he said.

I wondered if Raynelle knew she was wearing a ring pried off the finger of a dead woman. "How long since your mama passed, Lud?"

"Seven years. She come up sick with tuberculosis after taking care of some miners down in Wallins. She told me they thought they had Black Lung, but it turnt out to be tuberculosis. They was the only two left after the rest of their family died of it. Folks call it consumption and say it's real catching."

What? I recalled Mr. Webster saying Miz Webster *and Mama* went to Wallins to take care of sick miners. And Raynelle said Mama was feeling peaked afore she run off. My mind was spinning.

"Didn't *my* mama go with her to take care of those miners?" I asked.

"I s'pose so," Lud said. "But your mama didn't git sick, did she?"

Mr. Webster come from the store's back room and asked if Lud had taken care of what I needed.

"Flour and soda," I said. "Lud jist told me that your wife passed from tuber . . . tuber . . ."

"Tuberculosis," Lud said.

"Ain't true," Mr. Webster said. "Miners she took care of was sick with tuberculosis, and when she come down sick, she reckoned that's what she had. But the doc said it weren't. Said tuberculosis takes time to claim its victims. Said Patsy must'a had some other ailment on account of she didn't die a slow death. And he said tuberculosis don't usually cause high fevers, but Patsy was hotter'n blazes. He said it might'a been influenza."

"All this time I thunk she died from tuberculosis," Lud said. "That's what she told me she had."

I almost felt sorry for Lud, him thinking one thing and finding out it weren't true. It was the sort of thing that happened to me over and over again.

I wondered what the truth was about Mama. I'd heard so many different tales.

Mr. Webster handed me a sack of flour and a box of baking soda. He plunked more change into my hand than I know he should'a, and give me a wink. "We's nearly family now," he said.

Them words should'a caused me another shiver, but the words about Miz Webster still had my mind a-spinning.

CHAPTER 46

TALKING
WITH
MR. PUTNEY

I come out onto the street and seen someone duck quick-like betwixt the Grocery and the Dry Goods. I didn't want to head up through the woods alone and give him a chance to foller me. How I wished Pick was around.

Jane Louise's house was down the hill, but like as not she wasn't speaking to me after the way I treated her at church on Sunday. If'n I tried to go into the Dry Goods, I'd have to pass by that place where the figure'd ducked into.

I looked up and down the street. Nobody in sight. I hurried across the street, trying to decide betwixt the blacksmith shop or Mr. Putney's office. If Mr. Putney fired Mr. Grayson all them years ago, likely Grayson wouldn't foller me there. I stood on the office porch, hoping someone would come out from betwixt them buildings, and it would jist be Miz Sparks or Mr. Clark or anybody except Mr. Grayson. But the figure didn't even stick out his head.

I knocked on Mr. Putney's office door, trying to figure out what I would say to him. Could I jist say I come to have another look at Mama's painting?

After a hollered "Come on in," I opened the door and stepped inside, giving one more look across the street afore closing it behind me.

Mr. Putney looked up from his desk and seemed surprised to see me. "Adabel Cutler, right? What can I do for you?"

"I'm sorry to bother ya, Mr. Putney," I said. "But . . . but I . . . I . . ." My eyes rested on Mama's painting. "I thunk might be ya could help me straighten out the thoughts in my head."

He stood up and pulled a chair over from the wall and motioned me to set.

He leaned on the edge of his desk and asked, "What's confusing you?"

I stammered out a few pieces of words before I put a whole string together. "Ya told me my mama bartered with ya for her painting. Kin ya tell me what she bartered for?"

His eyes searched my face, as though he wasn't sure he ought'a tell me. My mind kept trying to sort out all its thoughts. Thoughts about Mama being peaked and Miz Webster thinking she had that tuber disease. Did Mama think so, too?

"Was it medicine?" I asked.

"Sounds like you knew the answer before you asked me."

"Was it medicine for tuber . . . tuber . . . consumption?"

"She didn't say what it was for, but she wanted tincture of opium and a few other things the store doesn't carry. Things most folks can't just buy."

Jist how sick was Mama? "And ya got them drugs for her?"

He nodded. "I did."

"Was she bad sick?" I swallowed a lump in my throat. "Was she dying?"

"No." Mr. Putney rose to his feet. "I don't think she was sick at all, just feeling a little puny from her condition."

"Ya mean on account'a she was goin' have a baby." Was me and Raynelle the onliest ones who hadn't known about the baby?

He nodded again. "She didn't say who the medicine was for, but I don't think it was for her."

"Who else would it be for?"

"Ray. Your daddy."

"Daddy?"

He set back on the corner of his desk. "She didn't say it was for Ray, but your daddy missed more than two months of work after I gave it to her. So it just seemed to add up."

Daddy missed that much work? How come? Was he really sick? "Are ya sure Daddy wasn't jist on a binge?" I asked, holding my breath a mite. Though more'n two months was a mighty long binge. Even for Daddy.

He put his hand on my shoulder. "I know your Daddy drinks, Adabel, but he never missed work on account of it. Never. And he don't drink on the job. I wouldn't'ta kept him on if he did."

I let out the breath I'd been holding. I'd been hearing folks say good things about Mama for months now. How nice—and discombobulating—it was to hear something good spoke about Daddy.

"Back then, I went up to your house to give Ray the pay I owed him, and he looked pretty bad. Wouldn't let me in the door. Said he didn't want me to catch anything. That's when I found out your mother had left, but I could never figure out why she left her husband when he was so sick."

The spinning in my head slowed down a mite. If Daddy was bad sick with something catching, that might explain why he sent us young'uns away. Might be Pick was wrong about him wanting to git shed of us.

CHAPTER 47

MORE'N A DREAM

I thanked Mr. Putney, leaving his office with my head full of questions. New questions. Was Daddy sick when Mama left? Or was she sick? And old questions. Why did she leave? And where did she go?

Standing on the office porch, I squinted to see betwixt the stores across the street. If Mr. Grayson was there, he was keeping well hid. I stepped off the porch right slow to see if a head poked out a-watching me. Nobody.

The Dry Goods door opened, and I jumped a mite until I seen it was Norris's mama. She looked to be heading home, so I hurried to fall into step aside her.

"Hey, Miz Shortwell," I said.

"How nice to see ya, Adabel. Ya ought'a stop by the house and pay Norris a visit. He's lonesome as a skunk-sprayed hound since yer brother lit out."

"Yes'm," I said with a nod. "Having Pick gone ain't easy on none of us."

"Him and Norris was close as brothers, ya know," she went on, as though I hadn't spoke.

Miz Shortwell was someone I hadn't asked about Mama yet. Since I didn't remember nothing, might be I could dig into her memory a mite. "The two of 'em was surely like brothers," I said, "when Pick stayed with y'all that time after my mama left."

"I know that was a horrible time for your daddy, Adabel. And you, of course. But we did enjoy having Pick around."

"You mean horrible on account'a Mama left?"

"That for certain, but I meant you being so sick and all."

Things tumbled around in my head again. Did I hear her right? "Me? Sick? I thunk Daddy was sick."

"That ain't the way I recall it," she said. "No, it waren't like that a'tall. Your daddy told me ya was bad sick, and he didn't want none of t'other young'uns to catch whatever ya had, so's he asked us to keep Pick for a spell—which we was glad to do. I think your granny kept your sisters."

"Yes'm. They stayed with Granny Cutler." Why didn't I remember none of what she said? Surely I'd remember being sick.

"Y'all was still in the old Cutler place back then. That house set so far off the trail, nobody even knew ya was sick. Or that your mama done left. Your daddy told me to keep it to myself lest folks be afeared ya had something real catching. And he kept hoping your mama'd come back. He'da gone off looking for her if'n *you* hadn't needed him so bad right here." She shook her head. "Them days was right hard on your daddy. I recollect him saying he near lost ya a handful'a times. Said ya was too weak to drink water from a cup or even take it off a spoon. He had to give ya a wet cloth to suck on to git water in ya a'tall. To try and git your fever down."

Miz Shortwell kept talking, but I didn't hear no more. My mind had stopped spinning and grabbed holt of her words about me sucking on a wet cloth.

My dream! The dream with the caring, gentle Daddy leaning over me and wiping my face. The dream where I woke up sucking rain from the sleeve of Pick's jacket. Might be it wasn't jist a dream. It could'a been a memory! Had I remembered something?

CHAPTER 48

MYRTLE HENRY'S SECRET

My ears stopped listening to Miz Shortwell. I kept thinking about that dream. That memory. If that's what it was. I searched my mind for the rest of that dream. Daddy'd spoke gentle words to me, words like in Mama's swing poem Pick had told me about. Was that a memory, too? Did Daddy recite poems to me when I was sick? Might be if I tried harder at night, I could dream other memories and fill in some of them empty places in my mind.

Miz Shortwell's voice caught my ears again. "Don't you fret, Adabel. It waren't your fault ya was sick. Your mama had jist left. Your poor daddy lost both her and the baby she was carrying in one day. So nearly losing you waren't the only thing that drove your daddy into the bottle."

Them words brought me out of my woolgathering with a thud. Was *I* the reason Daddy drank?

At mealtime, I watched Daddy close, looking for the caring Daddy from my dream. Or memory. But Daddy didn't make it an easy search. Some days, he was gruff and mean-tempered. Other days, he was hungover and quiet.

The next night, we ate supper without him. Raynelle kept a plate on the warming shelf above the cook stove, waiting for him to stumble home with a snootful. That snootful and all the ones afore it was on account'a me being sick and Mama leaving.

I watched Raynelle eat, and seen that my plate and Blissie's held more'n hers. How long had she been eating like Job's turkey so's the rest of us could have more?

"Ya ought'a eat Daddy's food since he ain't here," I told her. But she wouldn't. I hadn't always noticed it afore, the things folks does to make do. Jane Louise chased after Chester Putney. Daddy drank. But Raynelle done without. And she was even goin' marry someone she didn't love, jist so's we could eat better.

Raynelle never talked about the things she give up. She jist done it. Now I wanted to do something to help. I reckoned if I was the cause for Daddy's drunkenness, I ought'a find a way to make it stop. But how? Only one answer come to mind.

The weather turned bitter cold, sending icy fingers under doors and around windows. Raynelle kept fires burning in the fireplace and cook stove both. And her teaching me to take over the household chores never let up.

"Red oak and hickory will burn hotter than most wood, but ya need to bank a slow-burning fire at bedtime."

I begged off from the lessons with a lie. "I'm out'a white thread for the hat and apron I'm making for Lula. I ought'a run to the Dry Goods while Blissie's at school."

"We's out'a white thread? Are ya sure?"

The half-full spool was in my pocket. "Sure as squirrels like nuts," I lied.

Her fingers dug through the sewing basket. "I thunk we had plenty, but it's good to see you working on your sewing. Might be I kin work on Lula's coat alongside ya."

With scrip in my pocket for thread we didn't need, I headed out into the cold, down the hill and across the board towards Smoke Ridge. But I turned off in the direction of Myrtle Henry's place. I was determined to face her and demand she stop selling moonshine to Daddy.

My mouth felt as dry as the dead leaves the wind scattered across the yard in front of her house. The same wind froze my nose, but didn't freeze my resolve. I tugged up the collar of Pick's old coat against the back of my neck and dug my hands deep into its pockets.

I stepped onto Miz Henry's porch. But after all my resolve and determination, the old biddy wasn't even home. I knocked my frozen knuckles near raw on her door.

If I didn't want a scolding from Raynelle, I'd best hurry and buy a spool of brand new thread and git on home. I'd have to face that lady moonshiner another time.

But a strange thing happened. As I come from the Dry Goods, I seen Myrtle Henry pushing out'a Mr. Webster's Grocery, using the box she was toting to open the door. A box crammed full of groceries. Selling 'shine must'a earned her a pile of money.

I didn't want to confront Myrtle right where folks could see and hear, so I reckoned I'd foller her back towards her house and bide my time.

But she didn't head towards home. She went in the opposite direction, down Schoolhouse Hill, towards Jane Louise's house. I follered at a distance and watched her. And dang if she didn't go straight to the Heckathorns' door and knock.

I hid behind a pine and waited a spell, pulling my legs up under my dress one at a time to keep 'em out'a the icy wind.

When Miz Henry come back out again, her hands was empty. No box of groceries. No wonder the Heckathorns lived better'n us. They was gitting charity from Myrtle Henry.

CHAPTER 49

MORE SECRETS

I recollected the day I offered to help Miz Henry tote her groceries home. She done refused and got snappish with me. Was them groceries headed for Jane Louise's house, too?

As Miz Henry started up the path, I traipsed after her, keeping far back so's she wouldn't see me or hear leaves crunching under my feet. I lost sight of her at the point where the trail towards our old house cut off. Something inside me made me think that was where she went. So I headed that way, too.

When the trees thinned out a mite, and I knew I was close to the clearing where the house was, I heard voices. Angry voices. I hung back and listened.

Miz Henry hollered about someone stealing her money, and a man's voice answered back.

"If there was money behind that sign, it was from illegal means," the voice said. "You planning to report me to the sheriff?" The voice was a familiar one, and it prickled my skin. Mr. Grayson!

I peeked one eye from behind a tree trunk. Mr. Grayson and Miz Henry was on the porch of our old house. Grayson tapped the toe of his shoe against the *For Sale or Rent* sign. "You been supplying miners with illegal moonshine. I could tell Putney."

"You cain't prove none of that," Miz Henry shot back. "None of them miners'll speak a word against me."

"But I can raise questions about miners who got rowdy and lawless under the influence of your brew." Was he talking about Daddy? Mr. Grayson's words was icy cold, and I near-about felt sorry for Miz Henry.

"My 'shine ain't the only brew in Smoke Ridge," Miz Henry argued.

"No," the icy tone said back, "but it's the brew that got a man shot last year."

"You're crazy!" Miz Henry's voice was angry, but there was something else in her words. Was it fear? Did Mr. Grayson really know that her moonshine got a man shot?

"Most folks think Bud Heckathorn was killed in the fight between miners and deputies down near Evarts last year," Mr. Grayson said. He was talking about Jane Louise's daddy.

Miz Henry looked nervous.

"There was a shootout for sure," Mr. Grayson went on. "Union sympathizers and riled miners bushwhacked deputies. Men were killed. But Bud Heckathorn wasn't one of them."

"I hear he got caught in the crossfire," Myrtle said.

"He did, did he? That's not what I heard."

"I don't know what ya think ya know, but it's best for his kinfolk to believe that's what happened."

"You mean instead of knowing Bud was shot robbing a grocery store in Evarts? He wasn't with the mobs that robbed so many of them, but one night he tried it on his own. A night when a store clerk was standing guard with a gun."

"Hard Times kin make a man go against his raising," Miz Henry said. "Bud waren't a bad sort."

"Not until he got tanked up on your moonshine. Drink can make a man mean, make him take dangerous chances. The store clerk got scared after he killed Bud. He and someone else moved the body away from the store. Being shot the same day as the ambush of the deputies was Providence."

"Bunk!" Myrtle said.

"You were part of covering up what really happened. To make sure your own illegal activities weren't blamed for it. I think the law calls it . . . *collusion*."

I didn't know what Mr. Grayson's big word meant, but it seemed to scare Miz Henry. Was he right about how Jane Louise's daddy got kilt? I knew firsthand what Myrtle Henry's moonshine could do to a man. Taking food to a family might ease a guilty conscience.

CHAPTER 50

THE SNAKE AND THE DOG

Mr. Grayson and Miz Henry glared at one another as the cold air nipped at my nose and ears and crept up my legs. I hadn't moved since I'd reached that spot. Now I was afeared to move, afeared of being caught. I'd come to say my piece to Myrtle Henry, but if either of 'em seen me now, they'd know I heard what I heard. But if I stayed, I'd freeze plumb to death.

Mr. Grayson finally spoke, calm and easy. "I don't suppose you have anything more to say about stolen money. Am I right, Myrtle?"

"Ya's a thieving snake, Grayson, and ya better hope ya never cross me when I'm toting my twelve-gauge."

Mr. Grayson laughed afore he clenched his jaw and said, "Don't threaten me, you old witch." Then he slithered off towards the hemlock grove, jist like the snake Miz Henry had called him.

When he was out'a sight, I waited for Myrtle Henry to leave, but when she moved, she moved in my direction.

I held my breath and kept as still as a rock.

"Did ya git ya an earful, Adabel?" Her voice come from behind me.

"I . . . I didn't mean to eavesdrop," I said. "I wanted to talk to you, but I didn't know that man would be here."

"And what did you want to talk to me about?" Her voice was colder than the air that swirled around us.

What I really wanted to do was turn tail and run home fast as I could, but I was here, and I might as well speak my piece. "I wanted to talk about my daddy," I said. "I know he gits his moonshine from ya, and I don't want ya to sell him no more."

Miz Henry spoke in an almost gentle tone, a tone I never thunk the old biddy was capable of. "Ray Cutler is a drunk, Adabel. And a drunk will drink. If I don't sell him my 'shine, he'll buy some'un else's. Or Jess Fraley's dandelion wine. Or even Harriet Bailey's homemade cough syrup."

I felt my resolve splintering like that old washstand Daddy kicked, but I knew I had to keep on. "Don't it bother ya none to know he took food from his family to trade ya corn for 'shine?"

She raised her nose in the air a bit. "That ain't my concern. Your daddy had this nice house to raise his family in until he quit showing up to work a few years back. Couldn't make his payments and got behind. Clarence Putney let him back in the mines, but then he took to drinking."

"But Daddy not showing up to work was on account'a me! I was sick and he had to take care of me."

"Not my concern," she said again. "A widow like me has to earn a living. Without selling 'shine, I would'a lost my property long ago. Now it puts food on my table."

"And on the Heckathorns' table," I said.

She ignored my words and kept on. "It puts money in the collection plate at church, too. I don't s'pose you Cutlers drop in so much as a nickel on Sunday morning. Pastor Justice has to have gasoline money for his machine or he cain't drive over here ever' month. My money does good things."

"And bad things." I crossed my arms in front of me. "Your moonshine makes my daddy do bad things, too."

"It ain't my fault what Ray Cutler does when he's drunk."

"Like it wasn't your fault what Mr. Heckathorn done?"

She squinted her eyes tight and spat her words. "You best never repeat none of what ya heard here today. I don't ask your daddy to buy my 'shine. He comes a-begging for it like a hungry hound dog."

Them words was like a slap. Ever'body knew Daddy drank, but the way she painted him was plumb ugly.

"If'n ya want your daddy to quit drinking, you best go straight to the dog."

CHAPTER 51

THE
BIBLE

When Saturday come around, Daddy was off somewheres, likely searching for something to ease his unquenchable thirst. I didn't reckon anything I said kept Miz Henry from selling to him, and she was right about it not stopping him. He'd find it elsewhere.

Raynelle told me to strip his bed and dust his room whilst he wasn't in it.

His sheets was filthy and smelt like God-only-knows-what-and-druther-forgit. I toted them to the wash pot Raynelle had boiling on the stove. "I think these had ought'a go straight in the fire," I said.

Raynelle dropped them in the soapy water and pushed them under with a stick. "Git the dusting done in there, and when ya's done, ya kin help me run these through the wringer. There's enough sun to damp-dry 'em, and I kin iron the damp out of 'em afore Daddy comes traipsing home."

I went back into Daddy's room with the dust cloth. I threw open the window to air the stink out'a the room. Cold rushed in and made me shiver, so I hurried through the task of dusting.

There wasn't much in Daddy's room to dust, except a small

chest of drawers. The family Bible set on top of the chest, and I opened the front cover and peeked inside. Handwrit names was scrawled on the first page. The Bible had been in Daddy's family a long time. The first few names was fixing to fade, and their dates was from the 1840s.

I run my finger down to the newer ones and seen Daddy's name. I seen his marriage date to Ada Pickens. Mama. No death date. But I knew that didn't mean she was alive. Daddy jist didn't know whether she was or not. None of us did.

I seen Raynelle's name, Pick's, and mine, with the years we was born. Then the baby Raynelle done told me about. *Jefferson Pickens Cutler.* The writing told the sad story in jist one line: *Born dead, August 2, 1921.* Blissie's name come next.

Them was the names of family, folks who belonged together on account'a we was kin. But the baby was dead. Mama was gone. And so was Pick. There wasn't a whole heap of family left. I turned my head lest a tear fall on one of them names.

I dried my eyes and looked back to the Bible. Mamaw Pickens's name wasn't there. But that didn't mean she was alive. There was no name a'tall. No birth year. No death year. Not Papaw's name nor dates neither. It took a minute to make sense of it. But, of course! This Bible was from Daddy's family. Mamaw and Papaw was Mama's kin.

I put the Bible in its place on the freshly dusted chest. Afore I headed to the kitchen to help Raynelle with the wringing, I turned back sudden. Daddy's other book was gone! The blue-bound book like the one I seen on the shelf at Jane Louise's. It'd always set here right smack on top of the Bible. What happened to Daddy's book? Could the one at Jane Louise's house be the same one? How could it'a got there?

After my recent encounter with Miz Henry, my mind jumped to her. Might Daddy have traded her the book for moonshine, and Myrtle give it to Jane Louise's mama along with the groceries?

My mind was spinning again.

CHAPTER 52

INTO THE FLAMES

Daddy's sheets was ironed and his bed made up, and supper simmered on the stove. The tired smell of boiled cabbage. Blissie fed the fire and set down in front of it cradling Lula. It was still hard not to see Pick there with his face in a book. The house was quiet, and I would'a finished up the Christmas apron for Blissie's doll if'n she hadn't been a-setting right there.

The sun had give way to a frigid day. Gray skies threatened rain, but never follered through. The storm that hit was Daddy. He banged through the door, the smell of moonshine clinging to him like skin. He staggered, stumbled, righted hisself, and staggered some more, ranting about "jars being too short."

"A man cain't git a decent amount of drink from them jars no more."

It looked to me like he'd got plenty.

I couldn't bear to see Daddy like that. Talking to Myrtle hadn't worked. I was goin' have to talk to Daddy. Or try to.

"Set down, Daddy," I said. "Raynelle made coffee."

"Coffee! Bah! I need something stronger'n coffee."

"Daddy, please."

He swung his hand out wide, but I jumped clean of his reach.

"Leave him be," Raynelle said. "He'll pass out soon enough. I jist hope he makes it to his bed first."

I had aired his room and changed his sheets for this?

"I need jist a little nip to warm me up," Daddy slurred. "It's cold in here, don't ya think?"

"You been nipping more'n enough, Daddy," I said.

Raynelle shushed me and watched Blissie throw another log in the fireplace. "It's goin' be a cold night. We need to bring in more wood. Give me a hand, Adabel."

Raynelle and me stepped out to the porch. We hadn't closed the door yet when—I ain't sure what happened behind us exactly. But I heard Daddy say something about Blissie had ought'a help us. Might be Blissie mumbled something. I ain't sure. But I heard Daddy's bellow. And Blissie's scream.

Things happened quick as we run back inside. I seen Blissie's face, leaning down close to the fire. Seen her reach out her hand. Right into the flames.

"Blissie! No!"

It was too late. Blissie's sleeve caught fire as she pulled back her hand, clutching a burning rag.

Not a rag. A rag doll. It was Lula.

CHAPTER 53

THE
WAIL

Raynelle snatched up a towel and throwed it over Blissie's arm and the burning Lula. "Hold still, Blissie," she pleaded.

Blissie whimpered as Raynelle patted and patted that towel until the fire was out.

"Let go the doll, Blissie!" Raynelle hollered.

It'd been merely seconds, but it seemed like hours, watching Raynelle smother the flames on Blissie's sleeve. Daddy tried to reach Blissie, but Raynelle ordered me to hold him back.

"Set down, Daddy. Ain't you caused enough harm already?" I pushed him onto a chair and he landed with a thump. He didn't push back. Jist set there with a stunned look on his face. He shook his head. "I didn't mean . . . I didn't want . . . I jist thunk she was too tied to that doll. It's my fault. It's all my fault." He got up out the chair and dropped to his knees. "Blissie!"

I stepped in front of him, kept him from seeing Raynelle move back the towel from Blissie's arm. The sleeve was burnt black. Or was that Blissie's skin?

"Fetch the doctor, Adabel," Raynelle said. "Now!"

I opened the door, and it was Daddy who throwed a coat

to me. I'd forgot one. It was his own coat. Daddy's. It smelled like moonshine and coal dust, but it kept out the wind that was whipping up considerable. I pulled the collar up over my ears, but that didn't shut out Daddy's wail.

The deep wail went on and on, ringing in my ears, echoing between the hills. "Bliiiissssieeeee!"

CHAPTER 54

THE AMBULANCE

I raced down the hill through the dark woods, sliding on the frozen ground, and crossed the board over the creek with one step. As I sped through Smoke Ridge and down Schoolhouse Hill, I didn't look at nothing but the road in front of me. Leastwise, what I could see of the road with no moon in the near-night sky.

The mine whistle was the way to bring someone a-running to fetch the doctor from down in Evarts. But I stopped quick-like afore I reached the mine entry. It was Saturday. No mine shifts today. No fire in the steam engine. No way to sound the whistle.

The emergency ambulance set near the mine entry, in case of an accident. I couldn't recall it ever moved from that spot. And I didn't know where the key was kept.

What could I do? Blissie needed a doctor right quick. Mr. Putney probably had the key to the ambulance. Or he could drive his Ford truck. I raced up the hill again to his office. I pounded and pounded on the door, but there was no answer. The office windows was dark. I reckoned with the mine closed, Mr. Putney was home in his big house up on Pine View Hill.

Who else had an automobile? I thunk about Mr. Danfield's

Model A that Corky drove me to Harlan in. I turned to go back down the hill. Corky lived clean on t'other side of the mine. I scurried like the fastest squirrel God ever created. The stitch in my side turned into a stabbing pain, but I didn't slow down.

Corky's mama answered my knock on their door. "Adabel? What'sa matter, child?"

I was so out of breath I couldn't git words out but one mouthful at a time. "Blissie. My sister. Burnt her arm. Bad. Needs a doctor."

Mr. Danfield didn't start up his Model A like I thunk he would. He sent Corky up to the blacksmith shop to fetch the ambulance key from Mr. Clark.

I set between the blacksmith and Mr. Danfield as the old ambulance rumbled to life. We drove along the hilly roads the same way me and Norris done a week ago. Folks spilled from shanty doorways as we pulled up to the front of ours.

As I reached for the door, it was opened in front of me by Norris. Both him and his mama was there. When me and the two men stepped into the room, it packed our small shanty full, with folks crowded around Blissie. I squeezed through to reach her.

Her face was pale against the rag rug in front of Mama's trunk, her eyes closed like she was . . . no, I could see her little chest moving up and down. She was breathing.

And a row of raw potatoes was lined up on her burnt arm. Daddy wasn't there.

A bad smell hung in the air, and made my eyes sting. Was that the smell of burnt flesh?

I looked Raynelle a question.

"Miz Shortwell said potatoes would help," she told me, her eyebrows saying she had her doubts.

174

That wasn't my question. I tried again and mouthed the word *Daddy*.

She tilted her head and rolled her eyes towards his room.

The men lifted Blissie onto a stretcher, toted her to the ambulance, and loaded her inside. They said one of us could ride inside with her, and Raynelle said she would.

"Kin I go, too?" I pleaded. "I could ride in front like I done afore. Please."

"Some'un needs to stay with Daddy," Raynelle whispered. "And not the Shortwells. It's got to be kin."

I watched the lights of the ambulance disappear down the road, carrying my sisters away. And I prayed right hard that no new death dates would be wrote in our family Bible anytime soon.

CHAPTER 55

SUPPER

I shut the front door and turned to Norris and his mama.

"Thank ya for coming," I said. "Thank ya for your help. I—"

I saw a black wad on the floor where Blissie'd been. The wad that used'a be Lula. I poked at it with my foot first, then bent to pick it up.

"What's that?" Miz Shortwell asked.

"Blissie's rag doll. She . . . she dropped it in the fire and tried to rescue it."

"Oh," Miz Shortwell said. "I reckon young'uns don't always realize what harm fire kin do."

I didn't feel wrong not telling what really happened. After all, I didn't see Daddy toss Lula in the fire with my own two eyes. Even though I knew he had.

Norris and his mama jist stood there like they was trying to figure out what to do next.

"Why don't you come over and take supper with us," Miz Shortwell invited.

"Thank ya, ma'am, but we already got supper here, and I need to look after my daddy."

She looked doubtful, but Norris steered her towards the door. He turned back to me. "Ya know ya kin come and git me if'n ya need to," he said. "Or if'n ya jist want to."

"I know. Thank ya, Norris."

When they was gone, I looked down at what had been Lula. Nothing left of Blissie's beloved doll but burnt batting and one foot to prove she had once existed. There'd be no saving her.

I went to the stove, where I realized the burnt smell that insulted my nose when I first come in wasn't Blissie's skin a'tall. It was the remains of our boiled cabbage on the stove. And it was as beyond saving as Lula was. I would'a laughed at my crazy thinking, but it weren't time for laughing.

I picked up the cabbage pot and emptied it over the back porch rail. Lonesome sniffed it and pawed it, but he had no liking for it neither.

I poked up the fire in the cook stove and put on some coffee to brew. I opened the cupboard door, searching for supper fixings, but it didn't look promising. There was flour, but no baked bread. There was dried beans, but none soaking to make shuck beans.

My eyes caught the sight of raw potatoes on the rag rug where Blissie'd been. The potatoes that was put on Blissie's burnt arm. I picked 'em up and set 'em on the table, but I knew I'd never be able to eat one of 'em. No matter how hungry I got.

I found a few soda crackers in a tin. And way up on the cupboard's top shelf set four jars of blackberry jam. Raynelle had made it from the berries Pick brung home that morning of the day he left. I knew she was saving 'em for special, but I had a hungry Daddy who needed food so's maybe he wouldn't go back out hunting another nip. I set a jar of jam on the table aside the cracker tin.

I knew I couldn't put it off no longer. I eased open the door of Daddy's room. He lay face down on his bed. On those fresh-washed, fresh-ironed sheets.

"Daddy," I whispered. "You awake?"

He turned his red face towards me. A red face smudged with tears. "Where's Blissie?" he asked.

"They done took her to the doctor," I said. "Me and you need to talk."

CHAPTER 56

A TALK WITH DADDY

I poured Daddy a third cup of coffee. After a spell, his words stopped slurring. "That was mighty good jam," he said, afore squinting to ask, "Where'd ya git it?"

"Raynelle made it. From berries Pick brung home. Right afore he left." I saw the sad on Daddy's face, but I wasn't goin' let him off so easy. "I mean to say, right afore you and your dad-blame brawling drove him off."

I braced myself for his anger, but Daddy didn't move, his gaze on the chair where Pick had always set. "I hated myself ever' second of that fight," he said. "Hated me more and more with ever' punch. I kept telling myself to stop. But I couldn't seem to do it. Drink does shameful things to a man. Don't never marry a drinking man, Adabel."

"Never. I promise. You know what Pick told me, Daddy? Right afore he left?"

He give his head a small shake.

"He said you love drink more'n you love us. More'n your own young'uns."

Daddy looked straight at me. "That ain't true. Ain't true a'tall. I don't love drinking. I hate it. I hate what it does to me. And I hate myself for doing it. The drink gits holt of me. And there's a devil in ever' drop that takes over me. Ya kin hate me all ya want. I don't blame ya. But I hate myself more."

Might be Daddy wanted me to say I didn't hate him. I didn't, but I couldn't say it jist then. "I seen ya stop drinking for a spell, Daddy. Right after . . . right after ya beat on Pick. But ya started up again. After Raynelle brung home that Quaker turkey. And after I traipsed off to Harlan."

"You went to Harlan?"

"I did. But that ain't what we's talking about right now."

"Don't sass me." His voice rose. "I'm still your father. You best remember that."

"I know. But I'm beginning to remember a different father. One what took care of me when I was sick. Why cain't ya be that Daddy again? Why cain't ya leave the drink alone? For always this time?"

His eyes showed surprise. "Ya recollect when ya was sick?" He reached out and grasped my two hands between his. "Ya never used'a remember that."

I felt the warmth from his hands. "It's jist coming back to me in dribs and drabs." I swallowed the big lump that had showed up in my throat. "Is my being sick what made ya drink?"

He give my hands a tight squeeze. "No. Don't never think that. A man what drinks don't need an excuse for doing it."

"But I remember the way ya was when I was sick, Daddy. Ya didn't drink. Ya wiped my forehead and recited poems to me. What happened to that Daddy?"

There was a glimpse of tears for a moment afore his green eyes looked into mine. "You was so sick, Adabel. You was afire with fever. I couldn't believe how hot your skin got. I thought ya was dead more'n once, but ya kept fighting your way back. You always was a fighter, Adabel."

"I reckon I got that from you."

His face looked stung by my words.

"Instead of fighting with your young'uns, Daddy, why don't ya use the fight in ya to fight off drinking?"

He let out a long, slow breath. "I wished it was that easy. Drink devils a man, convinces him that one little nip won't hurt nothing. But it don't never stop at one little nip, even though I tell myself over and over it will. The second nip comes easier. And the third easier still. After that . . ." He shook his head fierce, his red hair flying all which-a-way, and dropped his face in his hands.

I touched his shoulder. "You said I was a fighter, Daddy. I'll help ya fight like ya helped me when I was sick."

Raising his head slowly, he took my hand again. "Drink has power. Ya don't understand what it kin do. You know them poems I read ya? I read 'em from a book I buyed for your mama." At the mention of Mama, his voice took on a sweet, sad, remembering sound that I didn't recall Daddy using afore. "She couldn't read," he said, "but I read 'em to her. She most favored one about a swing."

That was the first I recollected hearing Daddy talk about Mama. Ever. I tried not to let the surprise show on my face on account'a I wanted to hear more.

But Daddy's tone changed to an angry one. "When I was plumb out'a drinking money, I sold that book to Putney's nephew. He paid me with cash money, not scrip. I spent most of it on 'shine. When I sobered up, I give the rest to Raynelle, so's I couldn't drink it away no more. But I had no right to sell that book. Wasn't mine to sell. It was your mama's."

I recollected the nickel Raynelle give me for lard. Must'a been from Mama's book. I told Daddy, "I reckon Chester Putney give that book to Jane Louise. I seen it at her house."

"I hope Jane Louise likes it like your mama done. It should'a been yours and Raynelle's. And it should'a been a lesson to me about what craving drink kin do, but I been a fool more times than not." He put his hand under my chin to make me look at him. "Ya know Pick was right about me trading the corn away."

I nodded. "To Miz Henry."

"You know about Myrtle Henry?"

"I seen her still, Daddy. I seen her making moonshine."

"Ya's a smart girl, Adabel. Some folks thunk ya was ignorant on account'a ya couldn't read so good, but I knew better."

Smart! Daddy called me *smart.* I didn't recall Daddy ever saying nothing like that about me. But I couldn't let his words hang there like a falsehood. "I do have trouble remembering things," I said. "And reading don't come easy."

"But that ain't ignorance. That's from your fever. It got so high for such a long time the doctor said it harmed your brain, made ya forgit things."

My mouth opened so wide a buzzard could'a flied inside it. "My fever? My fever's what made me forgit all them things?" There was a reason for it. A reason for all the forgitting. I threw my arms around Daddy and hugged him so tight I dang near squished the life clean out of him.

I kissed his cheek and whispered in his ear. "I meant what I said, Daddy. If you fight, I'll fight with ya."

He patted my back in answer.

"Ya know Raynelle's planning to marry Lud Webster," I said. "With Pick gone, that'll leave jist you and me here. You and me and . . ." I couldn't bring myself to say Blissie's name.

Surely Blissie would be all right, would git better and come home. I couldn't let myself believe nothing else.

CHAPTER 57

SISTERS

I lay in bed that night, unable to sleep. I was used'a my sisters lying in bed with me. The bed was so big without 'em.

I heard Daddy scream out in his sleep for Blissie. I went in to calm him down. Between the blame he was feeling and the intoxication he wasn't, gitting him to fall asleep wasn't easy. I set with him most'a the night.

I told him I knew it would be hard for him not to drink, but I asked him to promise anyhow.

"I kin only promise to *try* not to," he said.

I went out to the kitchen and fetched the burnt tangle that used'a be Lula. I put it in his hand and said, "Keep this to remind ya what your drinking does."

Raynelle sent word that Blissie was in the hospital down to Harlan. It was Monday morning, a mine-shift day for Daddy, afore Raynelle showed up at the shanty again.

"I come in on the coal train," she said. "And I'm going right back on the night train. I'll pack me a spare dress and underwear. I'm staying down there."

"And Blissie?"

"She won't be home no time soon. She hurts considerable, but she's alive. They tell me her arm will carry scars, but her hand is the worst of it. If only she'da dropped Lula. She cries for her, you know. Cries for Lula. She don't ask for you nor me. Only for her doll."

"Kin I go see her?"

She shook her head. "Daddy needs ya here. And they want Blissie to git plenty'a rest anyhow. I spend most'a my time in a waiting room, until the nurse says I kin talk to her for a short spell. I'm hoping I kin spend more time with her on Christmas."

"Christmas?" I'd plumb forgot all about Christmas.

"It's jist six days away," she said.

"And I got nothing for her," I said. "Nothing but a half-made apron and hat for a doll that's ashes."

"We have to put off Christmas until Blissie's well."

"Oh, Raynelle. It's too sad. A Christmas without Pick. You and Blissie at a hospital down in Harlan. And I thunk Hard Times was jist about money. This here is the true Hard Times."

Me and Raynelle set at the table most of the day, talking more like sisters than we had in longer'n I could recollect. I told her what Daddy said.

"I done heard Daddy's promises afore," she said. "Ya's goin' end up disappointed if'n ya think he'll quit drinking."

"Maybe so. But I need to give Daddy a chance. Did ya know he saved my life? Back when you and Blissie stayed with Granny Cutler." I told her about being sick and Daddy taking care of me. "Daddy had a good reason to send ya away. Not jist for ya to learn from Granny. He didn't want ya gitting sick like me. Pick thunk Daddy done it to git shed of y'all."

"Pick always did find Daddy's worst side. Them two was like bucks in the forest, ramming their antlers up against one another." Raynelle took a deep breath. "Me and Lud are putting off our wedding until Blissie is well."

Not long ago, that delay would'a made me smile, but there wasn't no smiles left in me.

"And after we's married, I think Blissie should live with me and Lud." Her words was the kind of firm that let me know there was no arguing on the subject. And I knew Blissie would be better off with Raynelle than with me and Daddy. But it was like the last piece of our family breaking apart. And then my life would have nothing but empty places.

CHAPTER 58

NEIGHBORS

Miz Shortwell dropped by at noontime with a pot of stew. "I wanted to do something to help," she said. "And the Fraleys sent bread." She asked about Blissie and set with us as we filled ourselves with stew and bread. The stew warmed us deep down while Raynelle told her what the doctor said.

After she left, another knock on the door brung Teacher Bromley. She fetched us a plate of cookies, and asked about Blissie. I pulled out a chair for the teacher and poured her a cup of coffee.

"I'm afraid she ain't goin' be back to school for quite a spell," Raynelle said, and she told the story again.

I made another pot of coffee, as Miz Bromley settled in.

"I hope Blissie won't forget too much of her schoolwork while she's healing," she said. "Like you did, Adabel."

She give me a sad, head-shaking look. "I recollect when you missed so much school all those years ago. You were out for more than two months. After being one of my best readers, you seemed to forget all you knew."

"Me? A good reader?" I told her what Daddy said about fever

causing my brain to forgit. Knowing didn't fix the empty places in my head, but having a reason for 'em being there made me feel a heap better about it.

If only there was a way to mend the empty places in our house. And in my heart.

After Teacher left, me and Raynelle stayed on at the table a spell, but she lit out afore the whistle sounded, wanting to catch the train back to Harlan—and Blissie. Her presence had a way of filling a room, and when she left, the small shanty felt big. And empty.

CHAPTER 59

ANSWERS

Daddy come straight home after his mine shift, and set down to supper with me.

"The stew's right tasty," he said. "Did Raynelle make it?"

"What makes ya think I didn't?"

"Ya's a smart girl, Adabel, but ya ain't no cook. I reckon you'll git better with time. Your mama did. She was none too handy with a skillet when we got married."

It felt good to hear words about Mama come from Daddy's lips. We young'uns had shied away from the subject for such a long time.

"Miz Shortwell brung the stew," I said. "And a loaf of bread from Miz Fraley. And Teacher Bromley brung cookies. It ain't charity, Daddy. It's jist neighborly."

He nodded and kept eating. I seen how sweat dripped off his face in the chilly room. And the way the spoon shook in his hand. I knew the want of a drink was weighing on him.

I set by his bed until he fell asleep. Lula's remains set beside the Bible, their stale, smoky smell a reminder to him.

My own reminder was in the empty bed, as I lay there without my sisters.

True to his promise, Daddy come straight home again the next day. His shaking at supper wasn't as bad, and there was no screaming in the night. But I did hear him pacing in his room hours afore sunup.

Wednesday was a no-mine-shift day. I talked to Daddy whilst he built up the fires in the morning, and he talked to me whilst I heated Miz Shortwell's stew and set the table. It give him something to do that wasn't drinking. And it give me something to do that wasn't thinking about my sisters being gone.

I thunk he'd forgot all about me letting it slip that I went to Harlan, but he brung it up when we set down to eat. He asked me why I went there, and I told him the whole story—except the part where I bartered my ride with Corky for a kiss.

"I don't like that ya went traipsing off with Corky Danfield," he said. "I don't reckon I been a proper daddy. I should'a kept an eye on my girls and teached 'em to stay out'a trouble. That's goin' end right now."

"Yes, Daddy," I said. "But ya cain't do that if'n ya's passed out drunk."

"I know. We's fighting the demon together, ain't we?"

I smiled. I was fixing to hang onto my daddy as best I could.

"Daddy," I said at the breakfast table. "Did Mama give ya medicine for me when I was sick?"

Daddy shook his head. "Ya didn't even git sick until after she done left."

"But Mr. Putney said she come to him for medicine, bartered one of her paintings for it. He thunk the medicine was for you."

"That don't make no sense, Adabel."

"Might be it does," I said. "I been thinking on it. Mama and Miz Webster cooked for some miners down in Wallins who had consumption. After they come back, Miz Webster thunk she had it. But the doctor told Mr. Webster it was probably influenza."

"Influenza," Daddy said. "That's likely what you had."

"What if Mama had influenza, too? Might be I'd already caught it from her afore she left. But what if Mama thunk she had consumption and that's what she got the medicine for? Might be she left so's none of us would catch it."

Daddy looked confused, and I could see him thinking through what I'd said. "That's the kind of thing your mama would'a done, Adabel. But she shouldn'ta jist up and left without a word. She had'a know how worried I'd be."

"Might be she was afeared ya'd make her stay."

Daddy clenched his jaw and nodded. "I could never understand her leaving, but ya could be right. She left to pertect us. But," he went on, "your mama would'a come home soon as she found out she didn't have consumption. Why didn't she come back to us?"

My voice went soft. "I kin only think of one reason, Daddy."

His eyes probed mine until that reason come to him, too.

His chin quivered.

"I had you to help me through the influenza," I said. "And still, I near died. Mr. Webster said his missus died from it. I don't reckon Mama survived. I think she's dead, Daddy."

191

CHAPTER 60

RETURNING THE STEWPOT

Daddy's days got better, and he split firewood and helped keep the fires going, so's I had time to keep house.

At mealtimes, we talked about Mama, both of us grieving her at long last. Even though I didn't remember her, I felt I was finally laying her to rest in my mind.

We finished off Miz Shortwell's stew on Wednesday, and I scrubbed her stewpot clean. I reckoned I'd return it to her on Thursday.

Daddy's nights got quieter, but I still had trouble sleeping all alone. I lay awake and thunk on things.

I thunk about Raynelle and Blissie. And Mama. And Pick. I thunk about the neighborliness of folks who brung us food in our hardest of Hard Times. Not ever'body looked down on us.

The Shortwells had been friends as far back as I could recall—and even further'n that. Pick and Norris had wore a path betwixt our old house and the Shortwell shanty long ago. From them keeping Pick when I was sick to Norris fetching me home the day I went to Harlan, they done good turns for us. I recollected that day Norris brung me home in Mr. Putney's truck. And that day on the cemetery road when he seemed so proud that Mr. Putney let him use his truck sometimes.

Mr. Putney's truck!

I set straight up in bed, my eyes wide open in the dark room. Did Norris have the truck that day Pick disappeared back in July? Had Norris drove Pick to wherever Pick went? Them two was closer'n two baby possums in their mama's pouch. It had to be.

My eyes adjusted to the dark, and I stared at the window, not seeing it. Did Norris know where Pick was all this time? And not told me? I wanted to git out'a bed and go to his house and throttle the truth out'a him.

I knew I had to wait until morning, but there was no way I could fall asleep.

Next morning, I was up and dressed afore Daddy come from his room to wash up at the sink.

"I need to fetch Miz Shortwell's stewpot to her," I said, heading towards the door.

"It's too early," Daddy said. "Wait till after breakfast."

How could I wait?

We had no hominy and no eggs, so I set a jar of blackberry jam and a couple slices of Miz Fraley's bread on the table betwixt me and Daddy. I could barely chew, but Daddy didn't seem to notice.

I toted our dishes and knife to the sink. "I'll wash the dishes when I git back from returning the stewpot," I told Daddy.

When Miz Shortwell opened the door, I thanked her for the stew. Afore she could close the door, I said, "T'other day ya said

I ought'a come by and visit Norris. Is he home?"

"He's milking the goat round back."

I slipped around their house to the shed and poked my head in the door. "Hey, Norris."

"Adabel, what brings ya here?"

I stepped inside the shed. "I was wondering how far back ya been using Mr. Putney's truck."

The look on his face was like a critter caught in a trap.

I moved closer to him. "Was ya using it back in July?"

He didn't look up, didn't say a word. I took that for my answer.

CHAPTER 61

NORRIS
TELLS

"Ya took Pick somewhere in it, didn't ya?" The sound of my voice made the goat edge away from Norris.

"Hush up, ya's scaring Tillie," Norris said.

I stood quiet whilst he milked, but my hands was on my hips and my foot was tapping the ground.

"Hurry up, Norris," I whispered. "We got talking to do."

Norris kept his eyes on the milking pail. "Do ya realize that you and my folks is the onliest ones what calls me Norris? To ever'body else, I'm Shovel."

"Norris is your name. And ya's trying to avoid answering my question."

"I kind'a reckoned ya call me Norris on account of ya like me better'n most folks."

"I'm fixing to call ya by some names ya won't like if'n ya don't tell me what I want to know."

He poured some feed in a trough for the goats and picked up the milk pail. "I was kind'a hoping ya do like me, on account of I like you."

I hoped I didn't blush, on account'a I was trying right hard to stay riled. "I only like folks what's honest with me," I said.

He grabbed holt of my hand, and his fingers was warm and a little sweaty. "I made a promise to my best friend, Adabel. I couldn't break my promise."

I pulled my hand away. "Ya know we been worried. How could ya not tell me?"

He set the milk pail on the ground by the back door. "I give ya a hint once."

"A hint?" I didn't remember no hint.

"I told ya he cares about his kin."

"That was s'posed to be a hint?"

He reached for my arm, but I ducked away.

"I couldn't come right out and tell ya nothing without betraying Pick."

"Things is different now," I said. "We need to tell Pick about Blissie."

He agreed, but added, "Pick ain't goin' like that I didn't keep a better eye on things. Afore he left, he told me to make sure y'all was all right."

I had plumb lost my patience, and my temper wasn't far behind. "Where is he, Norris?"

"Like I hinted, Pick went to stay with kin."

"What kin? We ain't got no kin." My voice squeaked.

"Are ya sure?"

"I'm about to scratch your eyes clean out'a your head if'n you don't tell me where my brother is."

He stammered and sighed real loud afore he spoke. "He went to your mama's mama."

"Mamaw Pickens? She's still alive?"

"He thunk so. Said Mr. Grayson told him where she lives."

My skin went gooseflesh. "Mr. Grayson! Him and Daddy hate each other. Why would he help Pick find Mamaw?" But even as I said them words, my mind was thinking through things.

If Mr. Grayson was the man that fancied Mama, like Miz Bailey said, and if Mamaw wanted Mama to marry him, might be they still kept in touch. In all his snooping around, Mr. Grayson might'a heard about Pick and Daddy's fight, so he told Pick where Mamaw was.

Or did Mamaw tell Mr. Grayson to send Pick to her? And might be she wanted me to come, too. Is that why the man follered me?

CHAPTER 62

WHERE PICK WENT

"You know how scary Mr. Grayson is, Norris. And you let him convince Pick to leave? What's wrong with you?" I punched him on the shoulder. Hard.

Norris ignored my punch and grabbed both my arms. He held 'em so tight it hurt. "Pick didn't need convinced. He wanted to git away from your daddy, and Mr. Grayson offered to take him to Mrs. Pickens. But Pick didn't trust him completely." He dropped his hands from my arms. "So I took him."

"Where is he, Norris?" I asked. "Where'd ya take Pick?"

He mumbled the answer under his breath. But he said it all the same. "Up to Letcher County, near Whitesburg."

"Ya should'a told me afore!"

"Pick's my best friend. I owed him my loyalty. He didn't want your daddy finding him. Ya cain't tell your daddy where he is."

Part of me wanted to run right straight to Letcher County and find Pick. But another part of me knew that's where Mr. Grayson lived. And I remembered my promise to Daddy. I had to stay with him. I never knew when the hankering might be too hard for him to fight off.

But I had to find Pick.

"Daddy quit drinking, Norris. Pick needs to know that. Ya need to tell him. Tell him to come home."

"Ya kin tell him about your daddy and Blissie both if'n ya go to Letcher County. I kin drive ya to where your mamaw lives. Mr. Putney'll let me take his truck. The mine'll be closed till after Christmas, and he's taking his missus to visit kin for the holidays. Going in his Packard. Won't need his truck."

I never wanted nothing so much as I wanted to drive to Mamaw's with Norris and find Pick. I hadn't seen my brother in more'n five months. It would be the best Christmas present ever!

But how could I leave Daddy after the promise I'd made?

I thunk for a few minutes on what Norris offered, all the time him studying on my face. I couldn't leave Daddy, but . . . surely there was some way . . . something I could do . . .

"Daddy ain't never goin' let me go, Norris," I said. "Not without him. He was powerful riled that I traipsed down to Harlan with Corky."

"Not as much as Pick'll be riled if'n we take your daddy along."

"Take Daddy along? Why, Norris, ain't that a clever idea!"

"No. No, it ain't." Norris shook his head. "Pick was firm on that. He didn't want his daddy knowing where he was."

"But that was the old Daddy, Norris. He's changed. Changed a whole heap, Norris."

"Stop saying my name."

"But, Norris, I thunk ya liked it, Norris."

"Stop it, Adabel. Ain't nothing ya say kin make me take your daddy to Letcher County."

CHAPTER 63

THE DRIVE

The road was bumpy as I set betwixt Norris and Daddy on the seat of Mr. Putney's truck. I'd had Norris write a note to Raynelle in case she come home afore we did. I propped it betwixt the salt and pepper shakers, where she couldn't miss it. The note didn't say where we was going, jist that we was taking a drive with Norris.

Norris told his mama to keep an eye on Lonesome for me, and make sure he had something to eat.

I didn't tell Daddy we was goin' look for Pick. If he got his hopes up and we didn't find Pick, I didn't want Daddy to take to the Mason jar again.

"Norris knows where Mamaw Pickens lives," I'd said. "We had ought'a tell her about Blissie."

"Your mamaw was a spiteful woman," Daddy said.

"Spiteful or no, she's kin. We had ought'a tell her. Blissie is her granddaughter."

I thunk Daddy was goin' climb right out'a that truck, even whilst it bumped along the road. "You don't know what your mamaw's like, Adabel. Spiteful don't begin to tell it. I never met a meaner, more deceitful, conniving, hateful woman than Leona Pickens. How she ever give birth to an angel like your mama is more'n I can figure."

On t'other side of me, Norris cut his eyes towards me and shook his head. If this didn't work, Norris would never speak to me again. Nor Pick neither. But Pick hadn't spoke to me anyhow in more'n five months.

❖

The truck clumb over one hill after t'other. Drove around the bigger hills, eventually heading more north than east. Atop one hill, the sun was smack dab over our heads, and we stopped to eat the sandwiches I'd made from the last of Miz Fraley's bread. I reckoned, sooner or later, Raynelle would notice the blackberry jam was down to two jars. But she had other things on her mind right now. And so did I.

Daddy had the fidgets, and I didn't know if it was on account'a the D.T.'s or the thought of seeing Mamaw again.

I patted his shoulder. "Ya kin do this, Daddy. I'm right here with ya."

❖

Norris slowed the truck as we come on a couple buildings setting close to the road. He squinted at 'em. One had a sign that said *Grayson and Son, Life and Property Insurance.*

"Grayson!" Daddy bellowed the name. "Ya brung me to Grayson's place?"

"This is where Grayson said Mrs. Pickens lives," Norris said.

I had trouble with a couple words on the sign, but I knew the first ones. "Mr. Grayson has a son?" I asked.

"No," Daddy said. "Royce Grayson *is* the son. He works with his daddy."

I didn't want to see one Grayson, much less two.

And was Mamaw here? What about Pick?

CHAPTER 64

MAMAW PICKENS

We all clumb down in front of the insurance office.

A woman threw open the office door and said, "Mr. Grayson ain't here right now, but if'n ya give me your . . . oh my Lord in Heaven! Ray Cutler!" The look on the woman's face showed shock. And a healthy dose of fear, too.

"Leona," Daddy said, matter-of-fact. "Didn't think I'd ever see your face again. Adabel, this is your Mamaw Pickens."

"Mamaw Grayson," she said. "I married Franklin Grayson."

She turned to me, and afore I could say a single word, fleshy arms squeezed around me and dang near hugged the stuffing out'a me. "Adabel. Dear, dear Adabel."

"Nice to meet ya, Mamaw," I mumbled into her ample bosom, whilst I tried to keep from suffocating.

"Sorry, child. It's jist so good to see ya! What there is of ya. It don't look like ya's had a decent meal in a right long time." She pinched my skinny arms and scorched Daddy with a look. "Nice to meet me? Don't ya remember your mamaw?" The look she give me was a considerable change from the one she give Daddy, reminding me a bit of the way Jane Louise could change, becoming her pretend self when it suited her fancy.

203

"Adabel was sick a few years back, Leona," Daddy said. "It left her skinny, and she don't remember much afore that time."

She took to hugging me again, but I finally wriggled free.

Daddy went on, "This here is Darrel Shortwell's son. Ya recollect—"

"Shovel Shortwell. I sure do. Him and Pick was like twins sewed together at the shoulders."

"Speaking of Pick," I began.

Mamaw glanced up the road and seemed a mite nervous. "Do ya want to step inside for a spell? Royce and Franklin ain't here right now."

The insurance office was small and kind'a reminded me of Mr. Putney's office, only more cluttered. Boxes, books, and file drawers was ever'where.

"Sorry for the mess," Mamaw said, as she lifted a pile of books off a chair, making space for 'em on the floor by scooting a pile of boxes with her foot. "Set yourself down, Adabel. I keep watch on the office whilst the men make sales calls."

"And when Royce comes to Smoke Ridge to scare my young'uns witless." Daddy stood tall and straight, his hands on his hips, and looked eye-to-eye with Mamaw.

"I don't know what you're talking about," Mamaw said. "If ya've come to pick a fight, ya might as well leave now."

I set on the edge of the chair, whilst Norris stood and shifted his weight from one foot to t'other.

"Don't worry," Daddy said. "We won't be here long. This was a mistake, Adabel. She don't need to know nothing about Blissie."

"What about Blissie?" Mamaw asked.

I swallowed hard. "Actually, ma'am, we come to find Pick."

"What?" Daddy roared, that single word trampling over Mamaw's "I don't know what you're talking about."

"I don't have no idea where Pick is," Mamaw repeated. "Ya had ought'a go."

"I brung Pick here last July," Norris said, looking at the back door afore his eyes swept slow across the messy room.

Mamaw shook her head. "You must be remembering crooked," she said.

"No, ma'am," Norris said, stepping across my feet to pick a book off the pile Mamaw'd set on the floor. "This here is Pick's book." I recognized the book, remembered it in Pick's hands as he read by the fire.

Mamaw reached for the book, but Norris kept holt of it. "One book is like the next," she said.

"I give him this book two Christmases ago." Norris flipped open the cover. "See? His name's wrote in it."

My heart thumped hard.

Daddy's head jerked up and his mouth fell open. "You want'a tell me how my boy Pick's book come to be here, Leona?"

CHAPTER 65

WHERE MAMA WENT

Mamaw stammered a mite afore she said, "Pick showed up here last summer wanting a place to stay." She turned to me. "You understand, don't ya, Adabel?" Her voice held a sickening sweetness I couldn't abide.

"Ya know where he is now?" Daddy asked.

The thumping from my heart was so loud, I nearly couldn't hear Mamaw's answer as she changed her voice back to a screechy one. "It don't matter where he is, Ray. He don't never want to see your sorry face ever again. Ever in his whole life, he said."

Daddy's face was tight. He had'a know she was telling the truth. Was he remembering the last time he seen Pick? When he'd beat him black and blue and bloody?

"Ya best be on your way afore he comes home," said Mamaw.

I jumped to my feet. "How could ya not let us know Pick was here? Ya had to know we was worried sick."

"Pick jist showed up at my door," Mamaw said. "I never asked him to come. But what else was he to do?"

Norris spoke up. "You mean you didn't send Mr. Grayson to Smoke Ridge to tell him he could make money working in the insurance office?"

206

"Royce is a growed man," Mamaw said. "I don't tell him what to do."

"But you was the one who always tried to set my loved ones against me, Leona," Daddy accused. "Ya tried to keep Ada from marrying me. Wanted her to marry Royce instead."

Mamaw's voice come back with a screech. "And if she'd married Royce, might be she'd still be alive!"

Was my face as shocked as Daddy's? He'd gone plumb ashen and looked like he was fixing to keel over. I forced myself to speak, trying to keep the quiver out'a my words. "Ya know for a fact that Mama's . . . dead?"

Mamaw didn't answer right off. She let out a couple breaths afore she spoke. "Ada sent word all them years ago that she was afeared she was sick. I had Royce tell her to come stay with me a spell. I wasn't scairt of catching nothing. She didn't want to slip off like she done, but she was bad sick and Royce convinced her it was for the best."

Daddy clutched at a pile of boxes, and I was afeared he'd pass out. "She told me she was sick on account'a the baby."

"Set down, Daddy," I said, giving him a gentle push to the chair I'd been in. "Mama come here, did she, ma'am?"

Another big breath from Mamaw. "Yes. Royce fetched her. In the dead of night. She was sick as the trash man's dog. I didn't think she was goin' git over it."

My heart leapt clean into my throat. "Did she? Git over it?" I squeaked out the words.

Mamaw's voice turned sad. "She did, for a spell. But her labor come on, and the childbirth waren't easy. In the end, it kilt her." Mamaw pulled a hankie out'a her sleeve and dabbed at her eyes.

I'd thunk Mama was dead, but now I reckoned it was certain,

207

and I was fixing to choke on a tight feeling in my throat.

"She didn't want'a keep it a secret, Ray," Mamaw went on, "but she reckoned if she told ya she was leaving, ya'da begged her to stay."

"I would'a," Daddy said in a voice that sounded like he had the same choked feeling I did. "No doubt. I would'a."

"And that would'a put you and your young'uns at risk of catching what she had. She thunk it was consumption, and she didn't want no one else to die from it." Mamaw raised her chin and puffed out her ample chest a bit. "But I was her mama, and mamas don't mind the risk."

Daddy looked down at his hands. "I wouldn'ta minded for myself neither, but the young'uns would'a been a worry." His face looked up slow. "Where'd ya bury her, Leona?"

"Down the road a piece."

"Tell me exact."

"I'll take ya there if'n ya want me to."

Daddy nodded.

Mamaw grabbed her hat and locked up the office afore she led us along the side of the road the opposite way from how we drove there.

We walked single-file. I watched the slump of Daddy's shoulders as I follered him and heard the sound of Norris's feet behind me. Daddy and I had already grieved Mama, and now we was fixing to go through it again.

And Daddy knew that Pick had run to Mamaw after the beating. And didn't want to see him. Could he face all this news without a nip?

208

CHAPTER 66

THE BIGGEST SECRET

We come on a small graveyard set behind an iron gate. Mamaw pushed open the gate with a creak, and commenced walking betwixt the graves. She stopped with her toes up against a stone that read, *Ada Pickens Cutler, beloved daughter and mother, 1893–1925.*

I noticed it didn't say "beloved wife" nowhere, and I reckon Daddy seen that, too.

Daddy bowed his head and folded his hands together like he was praying. Mamaw watched his face, and that look of fear come back on hers.

"Why didn't ya send word she died, Leona?" I could tell Daddy was having a hard time holding on to his temper. Mamaw had to see it, too.

"And what about the baby?" Daddy asked. "Is it buried here with her? Or does it have its own stone?"

"Was it a brother or a sister?" I asked.

"A boy." Mamaw said. "She lived long enough to give him a name. Called him Raymond."

"For you, Daddy," I said. "She named him for you."

"Why don't we go back to the office and I kin make coffee

for y'all," Mamaw offered, behaving all nice again. "It's a long trip back the way ya come."

Daddy's eyes picked through the grass around Mama's stone. "Where's the boy's grave?"

Mamaw let out her breath. She looked around her, as though she was trying to remember. She looked clean up the road and back, afore she led us to the deepest part of the cemetery.

Far away from the iron gate and the road, she walked amidst gravestones, searching. It didn't feel right, this searching. Why wasn't the baby buried by Mama?

Mamaw's eyes seemed to drift back to the road more'n once. She'd led us to Mama's grave without a thought. Why didn't she know where the baby was buried? Did she only visit Mama's grave and never that of her baby grandson?

She stopped quick, beside a stone with faded writing on it. *Baby Boy* was the only words on the stone.

"Ya didn't put his name on the grave?" I asked. "Even though Mama named him Raymond?" Did Mamaw hate Daddy so much that she couldn't bring herself to put his name on this child's grave?

Mamaw hemmed and hawed and stuttered and stammered.

Daddy didn't question what Mamaw said, but Norris did. "This looks like a' old grave. The writing don't seem jist seven years old."

More stammering from Mamaw. "We got it cheap," she said.

"How come ya buried him so far away from Mama?" I asked.

"There wasn't no room by Ada."

I looked at the writing on the graves around this Baby Boy. *Henry Norton. Anna Dalton Norton. Charles P. Norton.* All with dates from nigh on a hundred years ago.

"How come Raymond's buried with all these Nortons?" I asked.

"It was the easiest place," Mamaw said. This time her glance definitely darted to the road. And my eyes follered it. Jist in time to see a hank of red hair pass by the iron gate. Pick!

"Pick!" I hollered his name and seen him turn towards the sound of my voice. "Pick!" I threaded my way around tombstones and headed towards my brother. I had to watch my step so I didn't trip over a stone, so I was clean to the gate afore I looked up and seen the shorter figure. A redheaded boy aside Pick. A boy who looked jist like a younger Pick.

It seemed to take a long time for sense to make it to my brain. But it did. And I knew. I had another brother! Raymond!

CHAPTER 67

RAYMOND

My legs felt wobbledy as Pick and me looked at each other. What would he do when he found out I brung Daddy here? I didn't say nothing, and him neither.

Until the others caught up. "Shovel, what in blazes—?" Pick sputtered.

"Shucks, Pick, your sister's like a dad-blame bloodhound."

"Sister?" the little boy said. "Are you my sister?"

"She is for a fact, Raymond," Pick said. "This is Adabel."

"Are you my brother?" Raymond asked Norris.

"No," Pick said. "This is the feller what used'a be my best friend. Afore I found you. Now we's best friends, ain't we, Raymond?" He ruffled the boy's hair.

Raymond smiled big afore he sidled over to Daddy. "Are you Pick's daddy? I never had no daddy."

Pick reached out to pull Raymond away, but stopped short.

I didn't know if Daddy was goin' pass out cold or strike Mamaw with his fist. His face leaned in to hers. "I have a son ya never told me about?" It wasn't a roar like the drinking Daddy would'a made, but his words were stern and crisp. Without a hint of slur.

He bent down to Raymond. "Yes, Son, you do have a daddy."

Mamaw turned away from Daddy. "Pick, you fetch Raymond home. These folks was jist leaving."

Norris tried to squeeze betwixt her and Pick, and I seen Daddy struggling to git holt of his temper.

"Ya don't need to talk to 'em," Mamaw said over Norris's shoulder. "Remember what your daddy done to ya?"

Pick's fingers brushed the side of his cheek, where a scar stood out against his freckles.

I stepped in front of him. "Daddy don't drink no more, Pick. He ain't the same as he was afore."

Pick didn't look like he believed me, but he scanned Daddy's face. He had to see the clear eyes.

"A drunk is a drunk is a drunk," Mamaw said.

"He changed!" I insisted.

"I'm *a-trying* to change," Daddy said. "Nothing's sure but the sun coming up in the morning."

"And it's fixing to set afore ya git back to Smoke Ridge," Mamaw said. "Ya best hurry along."

"Calm down, Leona," Daddy said. "There's things we need to talk about."

"And things we need to tell Pick," I added. "Give us time to talk a spell."

We walked back to Mr. Putney's truck, and the spell we talked was a long one.

"Ada would'a wanted me to know about the baby," Daddy said. "About Raymond. Especially if she give him my name." He run his hand along the boy's shoulder. "Why didn't she send word?"

"She writ ya a letter when she got well, Ray," Mamaw said, "asking ya to come and fetch her. But ya never did."

Me and Pick looked at each other.

"Ya say Mama wrote a letter?" I asked.

Mamaw nodded.

"Mama didn't know how to write, did she, Pick?"

I could see anger brewing in Pick's eyes.

"Did I say Ada writ a letter? That ain't what I meant. I writ it for her. That's right. That's what I done."

"I never got no letter," Daddy said.

"Royce took it to your house, but ya wasn't home." Mamaw said. "He left it for ya, but it must'a blew away or something."

"When would that'a been, Leona?"

Mamaw thunk so hard sweat broke out on her forehead, even in the December air. "It would'a been August 1925. That's right. August. Raymond was born in September. Day afore Ada passed."

I seen Daddy clench and unclench his hands. "What kind'a fool ya take me for, Leona? I wasn't gone from my house for a single minute that August," he said. "September neither. Adabel was sick, and I was with her ever' minute." Daddy looked like he wanted to wring Mamaw's neck like a suppertime chicken, and for once, I almost wanted to see his fist fly out, but he looked down at Raymond and kept his hands at his sides.

"Mamaw." Pick's tone was harsh. "Ya said Daddy didn't care about Mama or Raymond. Ya lied to me! Ya lied to all of us!"

"No, Pick, ya's wrong. I sent a letter with Royce. It ain't my fault if'n your daddy didn't git it. The bad blood betwixt him and Royce is his own doing."

I wondered if there'd ever been a letter. Likely Mama told her mama to write one, and waited to hear back. Or waited for Daddy to come for her. It must'a broke her heart that he didn't.

I knew we couldn't trust neither Mamaw nor Mr. Grayson. Might be if Daddy'd got a letter and knew where Mama went and why she left, he wouldn'ta started drinking in the first place. And if he'da knew about Raymond . . . who knows how different our lives might'a been.

CHAPTER 68

GRAYSON AND DADDY

Things went quiet as we stood in the crisp December air. We all had a lot to think on. I was surprised by how calm Daddy stayed. Knowing he'd missed Mama's last days and the birth of their son had to be weighing heavy in his chest.

Raymond's eyes never left Daddy's face.

And Pick? Daddy'd beat him, and Mamaw'd lied to him. Did he feel empty and betrayed? Norris put his hand on Pick's shoulder, but not a word was spoke.

The silence was finally broke by the sound of an automobile chugging up the hill. A Buick pulled over the rise, the sun glinting off its shiny chassis. It stopped right behind Mr. Putney's truck. My breath caught in my throat as Royce Grayson stepped out.

His suit and shoes was near as clean as his auto, and he strode over to where we stood. "Everything all right, Leona?" he asked.

"Chickens has come home to roost," Mamaw said, shaking her head slow.

Mr. Grayson turnt to Daddy. "Surely you aren't going to make trouble here, Ray."

The vein in Daddy's forehead stood out like a wiggle-worm on a hook, and his voice was loud. "We was jist trying to sort out all the lies that's been told and the secrets that's been kept." Watching his fists double, I plumb forgot how to breathe. "Ya kept me from finding my Ada when she needed me. And ya kept my son a secret." The worm-vein pulsed as Daddy spoke.

"I'm sure you're mistaken," Grayson said, pulling hisself up tall. He looked at Mamaw.

"They know," she said. "The truth is out."

Grayson turned back to Daddy. "No harm was meant. We had to protect your family from you. You can be a vicious man when you drink, Ray." I took a bit of joy in hearing fear in his tone.

"I didn't drink in them days," Daddy said. "Ya know that."

"No need to get upset, Ray." Mr. Grayson laid his hand on Daddy's shoulder like they was friends.

I waited for Daddy's fist to fly out, but all's he did was brush the hand off his shoulder. "There's reason enough for me to pound you to pieces and stomp on the remains," Daddy's voice roared, and then come back calm: "But my young'uns is here, and they don't need to see nothing like that."

I saw the stunned look on Pick's face at Daddy's restraint.

"Ya's been a liar and a cheat for more'n twenty years," Daddy said. "And Smoke Ridge is better off if'n ya never show your face there again."

Mr. Grayson's bluster crumpled a mite, and he edged towards his Buick. "There isn't much business in that God-forsaken coal camp anyway," he said. "I have to go where I can make money."

Without a look back, he clumb in his auto and drove away.

CHAPTER 69

A GIFT FOR BLISSIE

"It's late," Mamaw said, as Mr. Grayson's Buick disappeared over the hill. "Raymond needs to go inside and git warm whilst I git supper to cooking. Y'all need to leave now."

"We ain't told Pick yet what we come to say," I said.

"Pick, Blissie's in the hospital. She got burnt fetching Lula from the fire." I didn't say how Lula got into the fire. Daddy hung his head, but didn't say nothing. This wasn't the time for full confessions.

Concern showed on Pick's face. "Is she goin' be all right?"

"She will be," Daddy said, "but it's goin' take some time. She's at the hospital in Harlan. Raynelle's with her."

Pick looked at me. "Raynelle must be sick with worry. Ya sure Blissie's goin' heal? Kin I go see her?"

"They's making her rest," I said. "But Raynelle gits in to see her from time to time. She hopes to be able to spend more time with her come Christmas."

"Is there something I could take Blissie for Christmas?" Pick asked.

Pick was talking about going to Harlan to see Blissie! "Only thing she wants is Lula," I said. "Raynelle says she calls for her all the time. But I know *you* would be the best Christmas present. She

218

used'a ask ever' day when ya's coming home. Might be seeing you would be enough to make her forgit her doll."

"Foolishness!" Mamaw said.

"Will ya come with us, Pick?" I said. "And bring Raymond?"

"Ya cain't all squeeze into that truck," Mamaw said. "And Raymond belongs here with me. Pick, too. Raymond's the last piece of Ada I got left."

Daddy's voice come out quiet and calm. "If Pick don't want'a come home, he has good reason. I never made it a pleasant place for him. But he's always welcome to come back. And Raymond b'longs with his family."

"Holt on a second," Pick said and leaned down to whisper in Raymond's ear. Raymond nodded and run into the building next to the office.

When Raymond was out'a earshot, Pick lit into the rest of us. "This here is the sorriest family I ever seen! Daddy, Raymond ain't never goin' see ya raise your hand—or your fist. I'll see to that."

"And Mamaw," he said to her, "I ain't goin' let Raymond hear no more'a your lies. It weren't right ya keeping him a secret from the rest'a the family. Ya made more trouble than ya know."

He raised his voice even louder. "Don't ya both see what ya done to this family? I'll decide what's best for Raymond from now on. Ya hear me?"

I thunk the whole county heard him.

"And you, Adabel, I told ya not to come looking for me. Yet here ya are." He turned to Norris. "I should'a known ya'd give in to her."

"But, Pick," I said. "What about Blissie? We had'a tell ya."

Pick held up his hand to shush me. "Raymond has school tomorrow. And I'll walk him there like always."

Mamaw bobbed her head up and down like a chicken.

219

"But for Christmas on Sunday, me and Raymond is going down to Harlan, so's he kin meet the rest'a his sisters. It's been much too long."

A smile spread clean across my face, but Mamaw sputtered like Mr. Danfield's Model A done when I tried to drive it out'a the mud.

"I'll bring Raymond for Christmas," Pick told me. "I promise." He hugged me tight, and whispered in my ear, "Mamaw's husband is a right nice man. He'll let me drive his auto down to Harlan."

My brother's hug made me feel better'n I had in a long while, and it was right hard to let go. When I did, he give Norris a friendly shove, and even shook Daddy's hand.

As we stood aside the truck, I squeezed Norris's hand and mouthed the words, "Thank you."

He grinned and leaned down to whisper in my ear. "I was right. Ya do like me."

I give his cheek a quick peck. "Maybe," I whispered back.

A minute later, Raymond trotted to the truck, carrying something he handed up to me. It was a doll—jist like Lula!

"Give that doll to Blissie," Pick said. "Mama made it when she first come here. Made it for the baby she was carrying. But Raymond here was never one much for dolls."

I felt tears a-running down both my cheeks as Daddy bent to give Raymond a hug, but I kept looking at Pick and Raymond and telling myself I'd see them again on Christmas. I didn't know what would happen after Christmas, but I felt seeds of hope growing in my chest.

Afore I clumb in the truck, I hugged my little brother for the first time ever.

CHAPTER 70

THE HOSPITAL

On Christmas morning, Norris drove me and Daddy to the hospital in Harlan. Afore he left to go back to Smoke Ridge to spend Christmas with his folks, I give him a kiss on his cheek. Not jist a peck this time.

"Thank ya, Norris," I told him. "Ya been a good friend. To Pick and to me."

He put his arms around me and kissed me on the mouth. Right in front of Daddy. Afore Daddy had a chance to say a word, Norris clumb in the truck and pulled away, calling "Merry Christmas" out the window as he drove away.

A nurse directed us down a long hall with doors along both sides. Raynelle stood outside one of 'em, surprised to see us.

"We come to spend Christmas with you and Blissie," Daddy said.

I handed the new Lula to Daddy. "I think this should come from you," I said.

Raynelle's mouth fell open. "Where'd ya git that? Who made it?"

221

"It was made by the same person who made the first Lula," I said to the stunned look on her face. "It's a right long story. We'll tell ya 'bout it later. Kin we see Blissie?"

"The nurse is dressing her burns. When she finishes, we kin go in."

Raynelle filled us in on Blissie's progress, which she said was going well.

"Ya likely need a good night's rest by now," Daddy said. "Ya ought'a come home with us."

Raynelle's look towards Daddy was cold. She talked mostly to me. "I been spending nights on a couch in the apartment of a couple nurses. They live jist down the street. Only a short walk. And they's nice ladies."

We didn't tell her about finding Pick. Or about Raymond. If Pick changed his mind about coming here for Christmas—or if Mamaw or Mr. Grayson changed it for him—we didn't want Raynelle ending up disappointed.

❖

As much as I'd tried to prepare myself, I wasn't ready to see Blissie. Her bed was one in a row of four, but only one other had someone in it. Blissie looked small in the big bed, its metal bedstead painted white. She lay against a white pillowcase, her face near as pale as it was. Her burnt arm was covered with a sheet, and pain stood out stark in her eyes.

But she smiled when she seen us—even Daddy. Or did she smile at the doll in Daddy's hands? She reached out for it with her good hand and stroked its face and rubbed its hand against her lip like she always done with the old Lula.

"Ya fixed her! Ya fixed her!" Blissie's smile grew big enough to hide her pain. "Raynelle, did you do this?"

"Not me," Raynelle said honestly.

"Ya know I cain't sew," I said.

Daddy shook his head. "I wished I could'a fixed her a thousand times, but it wasn't me."

"Then who?"

"It's a gift from someone special," I said. "After all, it's Christmas."

CHAPTER 71

MERRY
CHRISTMAS

The sweetness that'd always been a part of Blissie didn't seem tarnished by her burns. She didn't hold no bitterness against Daddy, though I couldn't say likewise for Raynelle.

I had trouble keeping my eyes off the door, watching for Pick and Raymond, but noontime come without no sign of 'em.

A nurse brung a colorless lunch on a tray for Blissie, but Blissie ate blackberry jam on bread I had packed from home, jist like the rest of us. The bread was from the first loaves I ever baked by my ownself, but nobody complained.

"This is the jam you made, Raynelle," I said, as thoughts of Pick sent my eyes again to the door.

"Ya looking for some'un?" Raynelle asked. "Ya's watching that door like ya's expecting Santa Claus."

"I jist ain't used to being in a hospital," I said. "Folks goes up and down that hall like mine cars on a busy work day."

❖

The afternoon was half gone, and I'd give up on Pick and Raymond. I reckoned Mamaw'd put her foot down about allowing 'em to leave. Would Pick let her do that? She might have say over what Raymond done, but not Pick. Might be Pick wouldn't come without Raymond. Or might be Mamaw's husband wouldn't let Pick use his auto. Pick said the man was right nice, but I wasn't sure I believed anymore in Pick's sense of who to trust.

A nurse brung Blissie some medicine, and we backed away from the bed to let the nurse by. I felt a hand on my shoulder and turned my head to see Raynelle's face lit up. When I turned further, I realized the hand on my shoulder was Pick's. I spun around to be hugged by one arm, while his other arm hugged Raynelle.

"I reckon now ya kin guess who I was looking for," I said to Raynelle.

"Where on earth . . . ? How did ya know?" Raynelle sputtered a mite.

"The automobile I borrowed from Mamaw's husband got a flat tire," he whispered, afore he crept up quiet to Blissie's bed.

When the nurse backed away, Blissie saw him. And nearly jumped clean out'a that bed.

"Pick! Did Santa bring ya, Pick?"

"'Course not. Ya's too old to believe that." Afore her face had time to fall, Pick went on, "But Santa did bring ya something. Or someone."

He pulled Raymond out from behind him. "This is your brother. I mean, our brother. Blissie, this is Raymond."

Blissie didn't even question how or why she suddenly had a new brother. She jist gave him her biggest smile. And Raynelle even warmed up to Daddy a mite when we told her what happened up in Letcher County.

As I looked around that hospital room, I smiled, too. I didn't know how long Pick would stay or if Daddy could stay sober or

225

not. Who knew how long the Hard Times would last and if we'd manage not to starve to death afore they ended? I didn't let myself think about Raynelle marrying Lud and taking Blissie away from us. I jist thought about that moment, and felt something like an invisible hug from a Mama I couldn't remember, a hug that seemed to wrap around us all.

And maybe, jist maybe, she'd left us a small boy to help fill the empty places.

Because coal was no longer available in the mountains, people deserted this coal camp near Evarts, Harlan County, Kentucky, in the late 1930s.

AUTHOR'S NOTE

Smoke Ridge and its inhabitants are fictional, but Harlan County is a real place that has depended on its coal mines since the early 1900s. I have been there seven times, visiting several different towns. The folks I met were welcoming and helpful.

I loved listening to the sweet lilt of the Kentucky accent, and I hope I have captured an essence of that in my version of the dialect. My husband and I both have relatives from areas of Kentucky, and it's a treat to hear their accents. It's also hard not to pick up a trace of the way they speak when we're together.

Coal-mining children from Harlan County, 1946

The Hard Times the Cutler family lived through were experienced by most of the United States in the early 1930s. It was a time known as the Great Depression. Stores and businesses went broke and shut their doors, and the closing of coal mines and the cutback of hours were real. Much of the bituminous coal mined in Kentucky and Tennessee was sent to coke ovens, where it was burned down into coke. The coke was used to fuel furnaces in steel plants. When the steel mills closed, the mines followed. As the fictional Pick said, "One body's Hard Times becomes ever'body's Hard Times after a spell."

The thefts in supermarkets, particularly in the town of Evarts, really happened. The Evarts A&P had its shelves nearly emptied two nights in a row by mobs with hungry families to feed. Records show that the Quakers actively distributed food to needy families in Harlan County and neighboring Bell County during the Depression.

Many miners joined the United Mine Workers of America around the time of the Great Depression, but mine owners could hire non-union miners more cheaply. And men with families to feed were desperate. An ambush on sheriff's deputies by disgruntled miners actually happened near Evarts in 1931. At least four men were killed, and the incident became known locally as the Battle of Evarts.

Coal camps like the fictional Smoke Ridge were company-owned, and the miners were paid in company scrip. They lived in company-owned houses, and the owners took the rent from the miners' pay. The owners could control the prices the miners paid for goods in the company-owned stores, which were the only place scrip was accepted. In most company-owned mines, miners had to buy all their own mining equipment, from picks and shovels to explosives to carbide for the lanterns they wore on their hats. It wasn't an easy life for mining families even before the Great Depression.

Each miner filled cars with the coal he mined, and was paid by the ton. The blacksmith and the checkweighman were important positions in a coal camp. The blacksmith kept the miners' tools sharpened and the checkweighman weighed each car of coal and made sure the right miner was given credit for it. Miners were

A coal operation in Harlan County, 1946—the tipple (the place where the coal ore is loaded onto cars), head house, and conveyor

Above: The checkweighman at the tipple, Harlan County, mid-1940s
Below: Harlan Country miners in the late summer of 1946

232

assigned numbered discs, which they hung on the cars of coal they mined. The number told the checkweighman which miner should be credited for that car. The checkweighman marked down the tonnage for each miner and hung the discs on a board for miners to claim and use again.

Black Lung was a common killer for coal miners, who breathed in coal dust every working day. I met several people who'd lost ancestors to Black Lung. Their deaths were preceded by prolonged breathing difficulties and coughing up blood.

Cave-ins and explosions were also a constant danger for miners. The Zero Mine disaster in Yancey really happened, on December 9, 1932, killing twenty-three miners including the six Massingill brothers and twelve African-American miners.

Prohibition was the law of the land in 1932. The Eighteenth Amendment to the U.S. Constitution, which was passed in 1920, banned the manufacture and sale of any drink with more than 0.5% alcohol.

The Twenty-first Amendment eventually repealed Prohibition in the United States. It was ratified in December 1933, one year after *Empty Places* ends. But even though alcohol was again legal, many counties chose to stay "dry," keeping it illegal there. Harlan County remained dry.

In 1932, people with "drinking problems" were laughed at and scorned. The word *alcoholism* hadn't yet come into common use and alcohol addiction was not recognized as a disease. Programs like Alcoholics Anonymous didn't exist.

The poem "The Swing" is from Robert Louis Stevenson's *A Child's Garden of Verses*, a book my mother introduced me to when I was a child.

Besides these historical facts I used for this story, inspiration for a couple of my fictional characters came from real people.

After my husband's mother lost several family members to tuberculosis, she feared she would also die from the horrible disease. She wasn't sick and didn't leave her family as Adabel's mama did, but she convinced her husband to move their family to a healthier climate in the Southwest.

While living in New Mexico, she gave birth to her seventh child, my husband. She suffered complications from childbirth and died when he was thirteen days old. Her oldest child, a daughter, became my husband's mother figure at the age of ten. Can you imagine being ten years old and having six younger siblings to take care of?

Although these women inspired my characters, Mama and Raynelle are fictional. And my father-in-law was neither a drinker nor abusive. However, like Daddy, he was a proud man who didn't believe in accepting charity, though he readily donated to numerous charities.

Our country thrived from its use of coal, which fueled steel mills, power plants, and even home furnaces and stoves. Thousands of miners toiled long hours to dig it from the earth. They lived a hard life. While coal is still mined today, the days of company-owned towns are gone. Machines help to dig the coal and haul it from the mines, and other equipment helps detect harmful gases. These inventions have helped to ease the burden on miners, and safety regulations have decreased the number of accidents that occur. But mining is still hard labor and dangerous.

ACKNOWLEDGMENTS

A novel is not just written. It begins as a spark of an idea, which is fanned into a story plan. That plan is researched and mapped out. Characters are created, molded, fully developed, and given voices. Scenes are crafted and built into chapters. A narrative is constructed, composed, goaded, guided, strengthened, tightened, deepened, rewritten, revised, and tweaked. I could not have done these things alone.

I am extremely grateful to everyone who helped me bring this book to life. It could not have happened without Kent Brown and the Highlights Foundation's writers' workshops, where I learned to dig deep beneath the surface to mine every ounce I could. My efforts were guided by faculty members there, including:

Rich Wallace, who can always find what's missing or not working, and steer me in the right direction.

Jerry Spinelli, who convinced me my dialect worked.

Jan Cheripko, who also gave helpful advice on dialect, and who can find metaphors in tomato plants.

Editor Carolyn Yoder, who always knows what needs more work and pushes me to rethink and strengthen.

My fellow writers at the workshops, who provided encouragement and friendship.

❖

Accuracy meant being able to enter Adabel's mind and see the world of Harlan County through her eyes. That required consultation with experts, and I need to thank:

Carson Camp, director of the Coke Ovens Museum in Dunlap, TN, and a direct descendant of a long line of coal miners, for sharing his knowledge of coal mining practices in the early twentieth century and for answering my endless questions.

The folks at the Kentucky Coal Mining Museum in Benham, KY, for showing me the life of a miner's family, and for their patience with answering still more questions.

The staff at Eckley Miners' Village in Eckley, PA, who showed me coal camp shanties, a company store, and a moonshine still.

Hugh Jordan, for showing me the old coke ovens and coal mining equipment in Dunlap, TN.

Patsy Clark, for her Southern wisdom and hospitality, and for her help with dialect.

Jim Johnson, expert on cars and trucks of the period, for introducing me to his 1928 Model A Ford.

❖

I must also thank:

My first readers: Andrea Cheng, Reene Clark, Sally Derby, Josephine Keenan, Mary Ann Rosswurm, Linda Leopold Strauss, Rebecca Turney, and Tracy VonderBrink, who found time in their busy schedules to read a rough draft of this novel.

Ann Treacy, whose long-distance phone calls convinced me to keep going, and who wouldn't let me give up.

Nora MacFarlane, who read an early version and scrutinized a later version, sending me immediate feedback.

Dave Richardson, who urged me to push my dialect further.

My Northern Kentucky critique group, who listened to chapter after chapter, commenting and encouraging through every step.

Most of all, I thank my husband, Jim, who drove me to the sites I visited for research, and who waited patiently while I dug up one more fact or took another picture of a moonshine still.

BIBLIOGRAPHY

BOOKS:

Dormandy, Thomas. *The White Death: A History of Tuberculosis.*
London: Hambledon and London, 2001.

Forester, William D. *Harlan County: The Turbulent Thirties.*
Self-published, 1986.

Freese, Barbara. *Coal: A Human History.* Cambridge, MA:
Perseus Publishing, 2003.

Fremon, David K. *The Great Depression in American History.*
Springfield, NJ: Enslow Publishers, 1997.

McAteer, J. Davitt. *Monongah: The Tragic Story of the Worst
Industrial Accident in U.S. History.* Morgantown, WV: West
Virginia University Press, 2007.

Watkins, T. H. *The Great Depression: America in the 1930s.*
Boston: Little, Brown, 1993.

NEWSPAPERS:

Middlesboro Daily News, December 10, 1932.

PICTURE CREDITS